Deadly Obsession

USA Today Bestselling Author

J.L. BECK
C. HALLMAN

1

Zane

Cinder blocks weigh my eyes down. I attempt to roll over but every muscle in my body tenses. It feels like I've been tossed off a ten-story building, landing flat on my back. Groaning into the air, my fingertips graze something soft, a sheet... or blanket. I don't know, but it's not cold or hard. Shifting, I realize I'm no longer on the cold concrete but somewhere else. Confusion clouds my mind.

"Shhh, the police are on their way. Everything is going to be okay. They'll find the person who shot you." A voice soothes, but that's not the effect it has on me, and instantly my eyes snap open. Frenzied, I look around the room. The smell of antiseptic assaults my senses, and I piece the puzzle together very quickly.

Hospital. I'm in the hospital. The same hospital where Christian left me in the parking garage to die. Joke's on him though, because I'm not going to die. At least not today. Pain erupts across my body, and my muscles protest as I push off the bed and stand on unsteady feet.

"Sir, you need to lie down!" The nurse rushes over to me, her eyes panicked but I pin her with a dark look that promises pain, and she stops in her tracks. I don't say shit as I walk out of the room, my body screaming at me, begging me to turn around and go lie down.

That's not an option. Dove needs me. *Fuck.* I failed her. I let him get to her. I can't imagine what he's doing to her right now. Touching her. Breaking her. She's too fragile for a man like Christian. Like thin glass, he'll shatter her with a single touch.

My heart thrashes in my chest. Revenge. I need it. I'll take it. I'll bathe in his fucking blood for touching her and if he does anything to her. If there is a single hair out of place on her head... I can't allow myself to think that.

Hobbling out of the hospital, I get a barrage of dirty looks and some shocked ones as I pass people. Looking down at my shirt, I realize the entire thing is soaked in blood. All I can do is shrug because I don't give a fuck. My side is burning with each step I take, and I'm dizzy as hell. If I'm going to be there to save Dove, to save us, then I'm going to need to find a way to get this bullet removed. As I walk—to where I have no fucking idea—I play over in my head what Christian told me.

The Castro's, the rival mob family to the Sergio's, is the reason he wants Dove dead. *But why?* Who is Dove to the Castro's? Gritting my teeth, I know exactly what I'm going to have to do and that I'm going to fucking hate every second of it. The last thing I want is to leave Dove in Christian's hands any longer than I have to, but even with the raged haze that surrounds my head, I know there isn't any way I can save her if I go in there guns blazing by myself.

I need weapons, a plan, and to get this goddamn bullet out of my side and stop the bleeding before I really do die. Which means I'll have to go to the Castro family. Sagging against a nearby wall, I squeeze my eyelids closed, and force myself to breathe through my nose. The pain in my side is nothing compared to the way my heart feels in my chest right now. Even though it's hard as hell, I force myself not to think about Dove in that instant. Shrugging out of my shirt, I take the fabric and press it against my side as hard as I can. My fist clenches and pain radiates across my skin. It feels like razor blades are slicing through my flesh, leaving deep cuts in their wake. My eyes flutter closed, and I force myself to think about anything but the pain. Shutting down is my only option right now.

Car. Weapon. Castro's. In that order. Pushing off the wall, I continue limping my way down to the car. By the time I reach the car, there is a sheen of sweat on my forehead, and my muscles are protesting with each and every step I take. Swallowing the pain down, I open the car door and slide inside. Sagging against the seat, I start up the car and lean over the center console ripping open the glove box.

Pulling out the gun that I keep there just in case, I check to see how many bullets I have and then place it down beside me. Backing out of the parking spot, the tires squeal as I take the twists and turns to get out of this labyrinth of a place.

Following the exit signs, I slam my foot against the gas pedal and drive out onto the street. The sound of a car horn pierces my ears, but I don't pay the driver any attention. I'm on a mission. Determined. I don't need directions to the Castro estate. As soon as Christian told me about his rivalry with them, I started keeping tabs on the family. Figuring out their schedules, where they live, how they spend their money and time.

Going to them might get me killed, but it's a risk I'm willing to take if there is even a chance that I'll be able to save Dove. I'll make any deal; kill anyone they want. There is nothing that I won't do, no one I won't hurt. I have to get her back. I have to save her.

No matter what happens to me, I have to make sure she survives. She is all that matters to me. If she dies, then I die.

The wound in my side pulses with its own heartbeat as I drive through the city and to the town over. My insides twist and twist until there is nothing but a knot of fear in my belly when I arrive at the gate of the Castro mansion. There is a twelve-foot wrought iron fence surrounding the place, and the fact that I'm going to have to haul my ass over that fence to get inside is not a welcoming feeling. My side is already screaming at me, might as well plunge a knife into the wound. Staring up at the fence, I cook up a plan, one that has a fifty percent chance of getting me killed. Walking up to the fence and ordering them to let me in isn't an option.

I'm going to need to cause a scene, force Matteo Castro to see me face to face. Driving a ways down the road, I pull off on a side road and stash the car in the trees. If they haven't spotted me on the security cameras yet, I'll be shocked as hell. Hobbling down the road, I force myself into a steady jog. The air outside is cold, and when it clashes with my heated skin, I shiver. I feel weak, so fucking weak, but I have to do this.

I need someone in my corner, and since Christian wants to go to war, I guess I'll be the one to bring it to his door. But first, I need to get Matteo on my side.

Reaching the edge of the fence on the property line, I gaze up at the mountain I'm going to have to climb. Exhaustion coats my insides, and I have to force myself to continue forward. *Think of Dove.* Off in the distance, something catches my eye. *Not something, someone.* Two men are headed right toward me. Beefy, muscled, and with guns strapped across their chests.

I'm in no position to fight. Hopefully, they don't kill me, because fuck, would that be a shit way for this to end.

"Either you have a death wish, or you have a fucking death wish." One of the men sneers when he gets closer. The fence is still between us, but I know that won't save me. If they wanted to kill me right now, they could.

"I need to speak to Matteo," I grit out.

The same guy who spoke moments ago lets out a bemused chuckle. "You *need* to speak to Matteo? Sorry, buddy, but that's not how this works. If the boss wants to see you, you'll know. Now get the fuck out of here." He makes a shoo motion with his hands, and if I wasn't in so much fucking pain, I'd grin.

My gun sits heavily in the waistband of my jeans, and I know as soon as I reach for it, they're going to shoot me. It's a risk I have to take though. Shooting one of them will definitely get me to Matteo. Dead or alive? Not sure.

Moving with agility I didn't even know was possible, I grab my gun and aim it at the guy that laughed at me.

"No hard feelings," I grunt as I pull the trigger. At the same time, his friend pulls a gun and shoots. The bullet rips through my shoulder and into the tender tissue. How much more blood can I lose before I die? My skin stings where the bullet lodges itself inside, and I stagger backward, my knees shaking. I can feel the ground coming into view. Who knew that the mighty would fall so hard? After all I've done, everything is crumbling to the ground. The man always killing and ending lives has finally been caught by karma.

Landing on the ground with a hard thud, all I can do is look up at the sky.

"Idiot," The guy who shot me growls as he walks over, his face coming into view. The toe of his boot collides with my ribcage and pain ricochets through my body. *Fuck.* "You got your wish. Looks like you'll be leaving via a body bag, after all."

Pain encompasses me, and I watch through heavy lids as he lifts his gun and pulls the trigger again. Another bullet sinking into my flesh, burning through muscle. Another bullet that I'd gladly take if it brings Dove back to me. Blackness and pain are all I feel as my eyes close for what I feel is going to be the very last time.

~

THE FIRST THING I notice when I come to is that I'm alive. *Scratch that.* I'm not alive. I've died and gone to hell. Actually, hell would be a vacation compared to what I'm dealing with right now. My entire body is like a flame, burning and pulsing, gushing gasoline on a never-ending spark of fire. Every muscle tightens as I struggle to make sense of what's going on.

"Welcome back, Zane," an unfamiliar voice says, and I twist in the direction of it. Finding nothing but darkness. It's then that I realize my wrists are handcuffed to the sides of the bed. The metal dinging with my sharp movement. Tugging on them to the point of pain, I grit my teeth as the metal digs into my skin. Slowly, everything starts to come into perspective. Looking down at my bare chest, I find I'm no longer bleeding. Each of the bullet holes that littered my chest are now clean, and the wound covered with gauze.

What the hell happened?

"You can say thank you at any time." There's that voice again, and it grates on every last fucking nerve ending. I didn't go through all this for nothing and every second that ticks by is another second that Dove could be somewhere hurting or worse...

"I need to talk to Matteo!" I growl.

"Well, it's your lucky fucking day, boy." Out of the shadows appears Matteo, the man I need to speak with. His honey-colored hair is slicked back, and his dark eyes are menacing, well, about as menacing as a small dog chewing on your ankle. "I don't really appreciate you shooting one of my men, but I suppose we're even since he took one shot, and you took three."

"Not that it matters, but I was shot when I got here. Your guy only shot me twice."

Matteo narrows his gaze, a smirk twisting his lips. "I see. Still, you deserved to be shot, showing up here and shooting one of my men. Hell, he should've killed you. I will say that I'm surprised that I finally get to meet the infamous Zane though. Hitman for the Sergio family. Did you know there is a bounty on your head?"

All I do is shrug. "I'm not here about the bounty, and if you want to hand me over to Christian, then do it. He has something of mine, and I want it back. You'd be doing me a favor anyway."

Matteo stares at me, just stares. "You know that's not how this works. Your balls must be the size of Texas if you think you can come in here and ask for my help."

At this point, I don't care about anything. All that matters is saving Dove, making sure she is safe, alive, and protected. "I'll tell you all of his secrets. Kill whoever you want. Do anything that you need. I just need some guns and manpower. That's all I'm asking for. It's not a marriage or relationship. It ain't shit. You help me. I will help you." I try not to sound as fucking weak and desperate as I feel, but I don't think there is much I can do about it at this point.

Matteo gets up from the spot he's perched on. "And why the fuck would I help you? I don't know anything about you, and the last thing I need is your help. I know the odds are stacked against you. As the hitman for the Sergio family, a family that is a rival of mine, that continues to fuck with my business, I should kill you. In fact, give me one good reason not to shoot you straight in the fucking head right now."

"I don't have one. All I have is the knowledge that Christian wanted you dead. You were next on my list. Now, if you aren't going to help me, then let me fucking go." I tug against the handcuffs again, my muscles burning with exhaustion. Matteo looks indifferent, and I wonder what the hell is going to happen next.

"What is it that he has that would tempt you to make a deal with the devil?" I swallow thickly, hating that I'm going to have to explain to him who Dove is to me. It's obvious I'll burn the entire world down for her, so there isn't any point in hiding that she is my biggest weakness. I've already exposed that myself.

"Dove. He has her. She is mine, and I want her back." I growl.

Matteo chuckles. "You want to start a war over a girl? Over some pussy, which you could get from any woman?"

"She isn't just anyone, and he's going to hurt her. I..." It kills me, rips me to fucking shreds to say my next set of words. All my life, I've vowed to be strong, to look death straight in the eyes and smile, but this isn't just about me anymore. Dove wasn't cut from the same cloth as me, and she can't handle this world. "Please, she is my entire world, and I...right now, I have nothing. I am a walking target, if I go in there to save her on my own, we're not getting out. You're my last chance..."

Matteo cocks his head to the side, drumming his fingers against his chin. "And why would he steal your precious little girlfriend?"

"Because he's been looking for her for ten years... I don't know why, but I know he plans to use her for something. He claims it's your fault that he wants her dead, but I haven't figured out the connection yet."

"Interesting...so this girl, he assumes I know her?"

I nod. "But we won't be able to figure out how or why until we get her back."

A spark of curiosity fills his eyes, and I know I've hooked him.

"Fine. I'll help, but you'll be indebted to me, Zane. Indebted till I say otherwise."

Hope springs in my chest. I don't care what it is, or what he needs me to do. I'll do it. All that matters is Dove. My sweet Dove.

"Fine, just help me find her."

2

Dove

My bones are aching, every muscle in my body is stiff. My whole body is sore, and there is a permanent crater, an ache in my chest, that's accompanied by a never-ending emptiness. I'm so exhausted, my body and mind.

I'm not sure how long I've been here or how much longer I can take this. There are no windows, and the single light bulb hanging from the ceiling is always on. Someone brings me food, but the times are not regular. I know because sometimes I'm so hungry, my stomach is rumbling, and a pit of pain fills my belly.

Of course, it's nothing compared to the pain of losing Zane... William. I still can't wrap my mind around it. How did I not see it before? How could I have been so blind? He wasn't the boy I thought died all those years ago, but he still made me feel safe all the same. I should have known. Now I've lost him all over again.

Wiping the tears off my cheek with the back on my hand, I stare at the same wall I've been looking at for the last few days. I've counted every brick, memorized every crack because I have nothing else to do. Nothing to keep me sane.

The room I've been kept in only holds a dirty mattress, a thin blanket, and a bucket in the corner for when no one is there to take me to the bathroom. So far, that's the only time I'm allowed out of my cell—to go to the bathroom down the hall. I know I'm in some basement, a heavily guarded basement, but that's pretty much all I know.

I still don't understand why Christian is keeping me here, why he wants me in the first place, or what he is going to do to me next. All I know is that it can't be good. The days blend together. Night and day. I'm terrified of the unknown. Of what's to come.

Pulling my knees up to my chest, I wrap my arms around them, hugging myself tightly as if that would somehow keep me from falling further apart. Letting myself sink down onto the mattress, I curl up in the fetal position.

The rusty springs beneath me dig into my side, but the pain is only minimal. Forcing it away, I close my eyes and try to pretend I'm somewhere else... anywhere else.

Funny to think how I felt like a prisoner in the apartment, Zane kept me in. The whole time I was there, I tried to get out. What I wouldn't give to be back there right now? To be locked away, safe and sound from the world. Locked away with Zane by my side.

Another sob wracks through my body, leaving me a shaking mess. A sound from outside my cell has me quieting down in an instant. I sit up straight and wipe away the tears with the back of my hand. If they come in, I don't want to look vulnerable. I'm not giving them the pleasure of seeing me cry. It's something small I'm holding on to, the one thing I'm not going to give up easily.

A key enters the lock, the mechanical of it fills my ears. The door is unlocked and opened a moment later, and one of the men who has been guarding me appears in the doorway.

"Time to come out and take a piss," he growls. "Unless you prefer to go in the bucket?"

It doesn't warrant a response. Pushing myself off the dirty mattress, I get up and walk toward him on shaky legs. He hasn't touched me, other than jerking me around by my arm when he takes me out of the cell. Which I'm thankful for, but the way he looks at me is enough to make shivers of disgust skate down my spine. Like I'm some piece of hanging meat that he'll eventually be able to take a bite of.

Creep.

He drags me down the hall and shoves me into the bathroom. I close the door behind me, grateful for the privacy. There is no window in here either, so it's not like I can go anywhere. I do my business quickly, so I have a minute to wash up, and because the last thing I want is for him to walk in on me with my pants down. I splash water on my face until he opens the door and wraps a mammoth hand around my arm, tugging me out of the closet-sized bathroom.

"Dinner will be here in a little bit. My men eat first, and you'll get the leftovers... if we have some. Unless you want to eat now? I'll let you sit on my lap, and you can eat all you want." He grins, and the look in his eyes tells me he is anything but joking. He's serious and while I'm hungry. I'm not hungry enough to take him up on that offer.

"I'll wait," I mumble.

The guy starts laughing like the whole thing is funny to him. I feel like anything but. I feel like screaming, crying, and destroying this place with my bare hands if I could.

His laughter is suddenly cut off when the sound of some commotion carries through the long hallway. I can't see anything, the brute's oversized body blocking my view, but I hear the ringing of guns off in the distance.

What the hell?

"Fucking shit!" The guy with the death grip on my upper arm growls as he starts walking faster, dragging me right along with him. He moves me like a rag doll, my legs barely making it possible for me to keep up with him.

Then something hits me. I'm not sure what it is, but I don't even think. I just react. Normally, I don't fight him, but something about this moment tells me I should. Digging my heels into the ground, I try to slow him down.

I start struggling in his hold, hoping to get away from him, but all he does is pick me up like I'm a stubborn child. He throws me into my cell, and I land on my back against the cold hard floor. My bones rattle, and the impact knocks the air out of my lungs.

The door is slammed shut before I can get back on my feet, and the guy walks away. It takes me a moment to stand up, but when I do, I rush to the door and hold my ear to it.

For the next few minutes, I hear men fighting, more guns going off, and then silence. When I don't hear anything at all for a few seconds, I realize that no matter what's happening, no matter who saves me, good or bad, I need to get out of here.

If they leave me here, I will starve to death in this cell. I can't die yet. I refuse to let my life amount to this.

"Help! I'm in here, please, help!" I yell at the top of my lungs while banging my fists against the metal door. It rattles only a little bit beneath my harsh raps. "Anyone, please! I'm begging you, please, save me!"

It feels like I've been banging on the door forever when I finally hear someone approaching. The footsteps are muffled through the door, but I know whoever it is, isn't going to be good. The door is unlocked, and I step back toward the center of the room. Even if I wanted to hide, I'd have nowhere to go.

The door swings open, and two large men curiously look into my cell.

"Who do we have here?" one of them asks, his eyes roam my body up and down like he is evaluating me. For what, I don't know, nor do I want to find out.

"Answer," the other one growls, more in disinterest than anything. "Who are you, and why are you here?"

"I-I'm no one. I work in an animal shelter. Some man kidnapped me and brought me here." I don't know why that is the first thing I reveal about myself. They don't care where I work or who I am. I can't think straight. My thoughts are swimming, and the words I grasp for seem to slip right through my fingers. "They just took me and have been holding me here since. I don't know why. I don't know who they're or what they want with me? Please, just let me go. Please." I try to make myself look as innocent and fragile as I can.

I'm desperate to escape this place, to feel sunlight on my skin, to be free. I need to find Zane. No way do I actually believe he's dead. I need to get out of this place. Away from these crazy criminals.

The two men look away from me and back at each other, engaging in some kind of silent conversation. Then the silence breaks and the one closest to me, yells down the hall, "Ivan, we've got an issue over here." I jump, startled by the darkness in his voice.

Oh god, are they going to kill me? What's going to happen next? Panic bubbles up inside of me, but neither of them makes a move toward me.

For a few moments, we all just stand there looking at each other until the man named Ivan joins the other two in the hallway.

As soon as I see him, I instinctively take another step back. It's like my body knows how dangerous this guy is. I thought the two men who opened my door were big, this Ivan guy looks like he could eat both of them for breakfast, and then me. Strangely, my eyes snag on a tattoo that is peeking out of his collar and winding up his neck. It makes him look even more intimidating, not that he needs it, his size and the harsh look on his face is enough.

Yes, they are definitely going to kill me.

"She says she works at the animal shelter; they took her and have been keeping her here. She doesn't know why," one of the men explains to this Ivan guy, who I'm assuming is their boss. Ivan stares down at me, and I try not to look like a cat that's ready to hiss and claw her way out of this room.

"Go, clear the rest of this place. I'll deal with this myself," Ivan growls, and I almost pee my pants right then.

The two men disappear from view, their heavy footfall getting further and further away, and all I can do is look at this mountain of a man filling the entire door frame and bite my tongue to stop myself from begging those other guys to come back.

"What's your name?" he asks softly, finally breaks the silence after staring at me like I'm a puzzle he can't figure out. His voice doesn't match his appearance one bit. He's like the devil but with a heavenly voice.

"Dove... Dove Miller," I stutter, trying to keep my voice even, though it doesn't seem to help.

"Look, Dove, here's what's going to happen. You're going to come with us until we can verify that you are who you say you are and that you don't know anything of importance to us. If you're telling the truth and you are no one and know nothing, then you'll be free to go... as long as you can keep your mouth shut."

"And if I don't?" I ask, even though I know I shouldn't.

Ivan looks at me blankly, there isn't a sliver of emotion in his eyes. "Let's not think about that right now."

Instantly, I feel as though I've been tossed into the ocean. I'm bleeding out. The sharks are circling in on me. Who will bite first? I should've listened to Zane. Should've believed him when he said there were far worse monsters in this world than him.

"Okay," I answer because what else am I going to say? No, just leave me here to die? That's not really an option.

Moving out of the doorway, he motions for me to exit, and just as my feet pass the threshold, he says, "If you run, I'll shoot you, and I really don't want to have to do that."

A second ago, I was tempted to run, to try and escape, but the threat in his words revealed the truth. If he had to, he really would shoot me. I choose not to run. Hopefully, it's not the biggest mistake of my life.

3

Zane

I t takes me a few days to heal up, which drives me batshit
crazy. My bullet wounds aren't completely healed, but they're
as good as it's going to get for now. I should be out there,
searching the globe for Dove, burning cities to the ground and
slaughtering people, not sitting in a bed, staring at my hands,
willing answers to appear out of thin air. However, I can't do a
damn thing without weapons and the information that Matteo
promised me.

He says he's got eyes and ears everywhere, and if Christian
makes one move, he'll know about it. So far, he hasn't done squat
shit because Matteo hasn't come to deliver any new information to
me. I shove out of the cot and come to stand, my boots scuff against
the marble floors. I hate this place. I hate that I'm stuck being
someone else's little bitch, but more than anything, I'm afraid.
Afraid of what's happening to Dove.

The thought of one of Christian's men putting their hands on
her. It makes me murderous. Clenching my fist, I dig my nails in my
palm. Rage simmers just below the surface. If I get the chance, I'll
kill him, draw out his death, make him wish, plead, and beg for
death.

"Knock, knock…" Matteo's voice reaches my ears, and I force myself to unclench my fist, sliding the mask of emotionlessness across my face before turning around to face the door. I've already exposed my biggest weakness, and the last thing I need is to expose my emotions further. I refuse to let him or anyone else know how close I am to losing my shit.

"I hope you have some information for me?"

Matteo doesn't look amused by the way I talk to him, but the way I see it, if he wanted to kill me, he would've done so already.

"I do, but I think it's important you realize just who it is that's calling the shots here." I withhold an eye roll. I'm not used to working with anyone, let alone someone that mirrors Christian to a T. I don't take orders. I've worked as a one-man team my entire life. Now, I'm being forced to take orders from some prick in a suit. All I want to do is find Dove, do this asshole's dirty work, and fucking leave this place behind.

"Tell me what I need to know…*please*," I grit out. Matteo smirks at me as if he enjoys seeing me grit pleasantries through my teeth. Little does he know; he'd be dead too if I didn't need him as badly as I do. I'm not about ass-kissing or becoming his best friend. I just want Dove, and I'll do whatever the fuck I have to do to get her back.

"That sounds much better… glad you cleaned up your attitude because I would've hated not sharing news about your little Dove."

Her name rolling off his tongue makes me want to slit his throat, but I withhold as a bubble of hope fills my belly.

"Where is she?" I demand and take a step toward him.

"An insider let me know that there was an ambush at one of Christian's secret compounds. We believe that's where they were holding Dove. I doubt she's still there as Xander Rossi's men were just seen leaving the place."

Xander Rossi. Fuck. More bad news. Slicing my fingers through my hair in both frustration and rage, I try and think, instead of reacting. Using my fists isn't going to help her right now. I need to think. But all I can think about is my sweet fucking Dove, how she was tossed from one cage to the next, landing now with the worse villain of all.

"What do we do?" I ask a moment later.

"*We?*" Matteo blinks, "*We* aren't doing shit. You are going to go there and check the place out, see what the hell happened, and if there is anything that was left behind. Maybe they did leave her there, who knows? I'll expect you to return though, and if you don't, well, let's just say there will be more than a bounty on your fucking head."

"I don't take orders from you." I clench my fist, ready to slug him in his arrogant face. I'm so close to losing it, to shutting down completely and going on a killing spree, that it's not even measurable at this point. And this fuckhead standing in front of me will be my first victim.

"You do if you want my help."

Like a volcano seconds from erupting, I shudder with a burning rage. Coming here was obviously a mistake. I don't know if Matteo is going to be worth all of this trouble. He's dangerous, yes, but what level, I haven't figured out yet.

"All I need is a gun and a car," I say without even looking at him.

"I can provide you with both of those things. I'm also sending two of my men with you. Can't have you trying to run off if she is there."

"Yeah, yeah, I know, I owe you, and I better return. Get it."

"I'm warning you, Zane, if you find the girl and hide her somewhere, or if you try and disappear, I will find you, and when I do..."

I look up, and most men would be cowering in fear from the look he's giving me, but I'm not most men. I'm not afraid of this fuckwad, but I am afraid of what he can do to Dove, or at the very least, what he'll try to do. Double-crossing him isn't something I want to do unless I absolutely have to. With no one in my corner and no other help, I'll have to wait for the perfect opportunity to leave.

"If she's there, I'll return with her."

His gaze hardens, almost like he's trying to see if I'll break under the pressure. Luckily, he has no clue what I'm truly capable of and the lengths I'll go to save the woman I love.

"I'm trusting you, Zane. Don't make me regret it."

I don't respond. Instead, I give him a blank look. I'm going to find Dove and kill every fucker that touched her if it's the last fucking thing that I do.

～

PUNCHING the GPS coordinates that Matteo gave me into the car, I rev the engine and leave his mansion—my prison—in the rearview mirror. My muscles are tense, and I'm ready for a fight. I'm consumed with the need to find Dove. All I can do is hope and pray that Xander left her there, though the likelihood is slim. Mercy isn't something that man shows, and I doubt he would just leave a vulnerable, beautiful woman alone to fend for herself. Grinding my teeth together, I try not to think of that bastard putting his hands on my Dove. The drive is a little over an hour, and I white knuckle the steering wheel the entire way.

I see the car with Matteo's goons following me the entire time. Useless idiots. Sending them is an insult more than anything. As if I couldn't take these two out if I wanted to.

As the miles tick down, knots of fear tighten in my belly. What if they hurt her? Raped her? What if she's broken, and I can't fix her? What if it's too late? The thoughts keep coming, suffocating me with fear. I need to get a grip, to focus, but the idea of finding Dove unsafe and hurt is enough to make me sick.

I slow the car as I turn onto the road where the compound is supposed to be. Off in the distance is a ten-foot fence surrounding a house. That must be it. The organ in my chest starts to gallop, beating a little faster the closer I get.

One would think a place such as this would be guarded, but I suppose there aren't any guards left. Knowing Christian, he probably went into hiding the moment the Rossi's ambushed him. I mean, he's always had me around to fight his battles, without me, I can't imagine he's going to be picking up a gun to protect himself or rid the world of his enemies. No hiding is more his style. Turning onto the road and driving through the beat-up gate, I spot two men lying on the ground. As I pass their bodies, the bullet holes in their foreheads confirm to me what I already knew. Everyone here is dead.

Closing in on the property, the feeling of dread consumes me. There are three more bodies lying on the lawn. I park the car and kill the engine. Then, I grab my gun and climb out of the SUV. I doubt I'll need it, but I'd rather have it than not.

The car with Matteo's men pulls up behind me, and the two guys get out of the car a moment later. I try to ignore their presence completely and concentrate on finding the woman I love.

I don't know what I expected when I showed up here, but it wasn't this. Crossing the lawn, I walk around the side of the house. There are more men, more dead bodies. Reaching the side door, I don't bother opening it since it's already kicked in.

As soon as I step inside, I smell it. Death. Blood. Mayhem. It's everywhere. It coats the walls, the floor, the air. There is only one thing in my mind as I walk down the hall... please, don't let her be dead.

Ignoring the bodies, and the smells assaulting my nose, I make a quick sweep of the house, checking every room as I go. Before I go into each room, I fear that I'll find her dead inside, lying between the other bodies. But over and over again, I find the rooms empty, a short burst of relief rushing through me every time.

Not finding her dead might be a relief, but not finding anything at all intensifies my anger. I need to find a clue, anything that will help me find her.

When I find a door that leads down into a basement, my heart skips a beat. Running down the steps, I'm desperate for something, anything. Before me is a long hallway, and as I start to walk down it, I find that there are cells on both sides. The space is far too quiet to have anyone in it. Still, I can't let the hope in my chest die.

My eyes scan each cell, looking for the slightest clue. I grow more and more disappointed as each cell leaves me with nothing. Reaching the last one, my heart leaps out of my throat, and I rush into the room, grabbing the thin jacket I gave Dove the day we left the bunker. It's lying on the floor next to a dirty mattress. There is a bucket in the corner of the room where she was most likely forced to piss. The place is... it makes my stomach churn. It's hell on Earth.

This is where they kept her? On a soiled mattress, in a cold and bare room. My Dove.

She doesn't belong in a place like this. She should be safe and happy. Scanning the room one last time, I note that there is no blood, and no clothing tossed aside, other than the jacket. Both are good signs, and I'm going to hold on to them. They don't prove that they didn't hurt her, but all I can do is hope that they didn't and that she's not completely broken when I get her back.

Fisting the material in my hand, I bring it to my nose and inhale deeply. The faint smell of vanilla tickles my nose, and I suck that precious scent deep into my lungs. She's a drug to my senses, to my mind, and body.

My sweet Dove.

At least I know one thing. Her not being here means that, at the very least, she is still alive. The question now, is how do I get her back from Xander Rossi, one of the most feared mafia men in the United States?

4

Dove

Ivan is quiet as he drives us to god knows where. I'm sandwiched in the back seat between the two guys that found me in my cell. I'm afraid to move, breathe, and damn well, too scared to talk. I do my best not to think about what's going to happen next. Surely, if that Ivan man was going to kill me, he would've done it back in that cell, right?

Of course, there are worse things than death...

A million and one scenarios play out in my mind. The car jerks to a stop, and I blink out of my thoughts, realizing we've arrived wherever it is that we were going. Peering out the windshield, I see a massive compound ahead. There's a ten-foot iron fence that cages the place in. It all but says no visitors welcome.

Two guards usher us in, and Ivan drives up the long driveway, past guard towers, and some smaller buildings. I guess escaping is out of the question.

In the center of the place is a giant house, or mansion even. It looks fancy. When we get closer, I see that there is yet another fence surrounding it. The lawn is manicured, and it doesn't seem like even a single blade is out of place. The gate in front of us is manned by four men, and I shiver, wondering where the hell it is they've brought me. Prison, but nicer?

It looks *nice* but kind of deadly too. We drive through the gate that leads to the mansion and down the road until we make it to a plain-looking building. I'm shaking, and there is a sheen of sweat on my forehead. Ivan shifts the car into park and kills the engine.

Ivan steps out of the car, and both men open their doors. One of the men wraps his hand around my wrist and pulls me out of the SUV. Shocked, I let out a gasp and tug my arm from his hand. I'm so tired of people grabbing me. Tired of being tossed around like a ragdoll.

"Don't touch the girl," Ivan orders, with a look so deadly, it makes my heart quake in my chest.

"It's not like I hurt her." The unknown guy shrugs his shoulders.

Ivan ignores him completely and starts walking away. My feet scrape against the concrete as I scurry behind him. I don't want to be stuck out here with these guys by myself.

"I'm glad you decided not to run," Ivan says and I almost roll my eyes. Where am I going to run to? He walks me to the large metal door. It looks like it weighs a ton, but of course, a man of his size opens it like it's a soda can. With the door open, he motions for me to go inside.

I'm not sure if I'm walking myself to my own execution or to a chat with an old friend. Either way, I'm not letting him see how scared I am. Forcing my arms to casually hang by my side, instead of wrapping them around my torso like I want to, like I need to, I walk into the building.

"That way," Ivan says and points down the hallway. The walls are bare, and everything from floor to ceiling is a light gray color. My shoes squeak against the floor as we walk. He leads me to a room that doesn't look any different than the hall, except that it holds a table and a few chairs in the center.

"Where are we?" I ask as I step into the room, gazing over my shoulder hesitantly.

"Sit," he orders, ignoring my question. "I have my guys checking on the story you told me right now, but in the meantime, I'd like to hear the whole thing again from you, and I'd like to ask you some questions. For instance, why were you at Christian's compound, and how long were you there?"

Sighing, I slump into the chair. I guess I'm being interrogated now.

For the next hour or so, I tell Ivan my story. I repeat the same thing three times. I tell him how they kidnapped me from the hospital. How they kept me in that cell. I tell him everything I can remember about my stay there. Every conversation I overheard. I describe every person I saw and anything else I can possibly remember, none of which gives a single clue as to why they were keeping me there in the first place.

By the time I'm nearly finished telling him the same story for the third time, my interrogation is interrupted by Ivan's phone ringing. He pulls it out of his pocket and looks at the screen before looking at me and back down again.

Ivan answers the phone with a grunt, then raises his eyebrows curiously when the person on the other side says something. I can hear a male voice coming through the receiver, but I can't make out what he is saying. I feel like a small child right now. My butt is sore, and my back is stiff from sitting on this plastic chair for so long. I'm exhausted, physically, and mentally, and all I want to do is to lie down somewhere and go to sleep.

"Got it, boss," he finally says and ends the call. "Well, this is going to be either really bad or really good for you."

Fear replaces the pain in my butt cheeks. "Huh? What does that mean?"

"The boss himself is going to come here and talk to you," Ivan explains.

Puzzled, I stare at him. "I thought you were the boss?"

"Not quite." A shiver runs down my spine at the thought of

meeting the man that has the power to order a guy like Ivan around. I chew on my bottom lip nervously as we wait in silence.

A few minutes later, I hear footsteps approaching from down the hall. I instinctively sit up a little straighter, wanting to seem less like a bug that this man can squish. Wringing my hands in my lap, I watch as the door opens, and a tall man, wearing a black tailored suit, appears. He's not as large as Ivan, but his dark eyes tell me he can cause just as much damage and mayhem... maybe even more than him.

His eyes are downcast, reading something on a paper he is holding as he steps into the room. He looks angry, almost furious, like he is about to yell at me, maybe beat me or worse.

"You interrupted my family dinner, little girl," he growls, his voice dripping with annoyance and hatred... hatred for me. He throws the stack of papers on the table in front of him and looks up at me.

Dark eyes connect with mine, and for a moment, I'm so scared, I forget to breathe. Then, something weird happens. An emotion I don't understand flickers in his gaze... pity? His eyes soften, but not much, and they swirl from pitch black to stormy cloud gray.

He takes the seat next to Ivan, never taking his eyes off of me. His stare is so intense, it makes me even more uncomfortable than I already am. It's like he's inspecting me, trying to figure me out. I do my best not to squirm in my seat, but that's a little hard with two of the most intimidating men I've ever seen sitting before me.

After an awkward moment of silence, he starts talking. "Dove, is it?"

"Yes," I answer before asking, "Who are you?" I don't know where this burst of confidence comes from, but I kind of like it.

He raises one of his eyebrows and leans back in his seat as if he is just getting comfortable. Maybe I should've kept my mouth shut. Screw my newfound confidence. That shit is going to get me killed. I need to be quiet like a mouse to get myself out of this.

His lips twitch up into the tiniest smile before he introduces himself. "Xander Rossi. And you, Dove, are at my compound. I expected you to tell Ivan the truth. We did save you after all, didn't we?"

"I didn't lie," I start to defend myself, but Xander holds up his hand, shutting me up.

"You told us you were kidnapped at the hospital, but your employer reported you missing a week prior to that. There was a police report stating that your apartment was broken into, nothing of value was taken, but it was ransacked like someone was looking for something."

"My apartment?" I question as if that's my biggest issue right now. "I-I can explain."

"Explain then," Xander growls a warning in his tone, "Better make it good."

"I didn't lie. Everything I said happened... I just didn't tell you what happened before that. I didn't think it would matter." I shrug. "And I really just didn't want to talk about that part." My lips tremble as I speak, and if I didn't want to make myself look weak, I was doing a really shitty job of it.

"What happened before?" Xander asks, cocking his head to the side as if the newfound angle well help decipher what I'm saying better.

"This is probably going to sound like a lie, but I swear it's not. I was kidnapped... twice. One time from my apartment and then a second time from the hospital, but the first time it wasn't Christian. It was..." I pause, wondering if I can tell this part without starting to cry. I don't want to, but tears are already dwelling in my eyes. Blinking the tears away, I continue, "His name was Zane. He kidnapped me first, but not to hurt me. He just wanted to keep me safe."

"Zane?" Xander says his name as if he's tasting it. He and Ivan exchange a glance, then he turns back to me and asks, "Who is Zane to you?"

"We both grew up in foster care. We were in the same home at one point. A bad one." My voice breaks at the end, and I'm no longer able to hold back the tears, no matter how hard I try. The memories of that time rush forward, the memory of him. William, Zane, how I lost him twice now. Unable to look at the two men, I lower my gaze and stare at a random speck on the table instead.

"Do you know where Zane is now?" Ivan is the one who speaks this time, his voice soft.

"He is dead." I start to sob. "Christian killed him."

"I think I can put the rest together myself. Christian must have taken you to get to Zane," Xander says.

"So, you believe me?" I glance up at him, hopeful that he is going to let me go.

"I do, but you did withhold information, and that's pretty close to lying." He starts tapping his finger against the table like he is thinking about what to do with me.

Please, don't kill me... "Ivan asked you to tell him everything, and you didn't. I don't like that. How can I be sure that you aren't still keeping things from me? I don't like liars, Dove, and I've killed men for lesser things."

"I'm not! I swear. I don't know anything else." The words spill from my lips, and I slam my knee against the table, attempting to get them out.

"How old are you?" Xander asks, changing the subject abruptly.

"Twenty-one," I tell him, wondering why he cares about my age. When he doesn't say anything else, I start to worry. I chew the inside of my cheek until I taste blood.

"Please, just let me go," I beg, in a last-ditch effort.

"I can't do that," he finally says, his voice clipped. "You're going to have to stay here, for now at least, until we get everything figured out."

"What? Why?" I stand up, having the sudden need to move. Or maybe for one second, I just want to feel bigger than the two men sitting in front of me. "You can't just keep me here. I'm not an object that can be taken and passed off to another person. I'm a human."

"I can, and I will." Xander gets up as well, turning his back to me. "Put her in one of the rooms back here. Have two guys posted in front of her door at all times. No one gets in this place without my permission."

"You got it." Ivan nods, and Xander disappears from the room, the imprint he made lingers behind like a heavy fog. "Come on, I'll bring you to your room."

"You mean prison?"

"Call it what you want, but it's a whole lot nicer than the shit-hole Christian kept you in."

"Great," I murmur under my breath. *It's still a prison.* We leave the room, and I follow him down the hallway, knowing that there is no use in trying to run. I saw the security outside this building. I wouldn't make it ten feet out there, without someone shooting me. Escape isn't an option at this point. I'll have to make do with what's here and come up with a plan later.

When we get to the very last door at the end of the hall, he opens it and waves me inside. To my surprise, I find that he wasn't lying. It is much nicer than my last cell, and no matter how bitter I am about still being a captive, this is a huge relief.

The room is small and doesn't hold much, but there is a bed inside. A bed with fresh sheets, a pillow, and a blanket. The second thing I notice is an attached bathroom.

Thank god.

"There is a shower in the bathroom. Towels and everything else you need should be there too. The closet has extra clothes. They're men's clothes, but they're clean."

"Thanks..." I murmur before I can stop myself. I shouldn't be thanking him for anything. Then again, I guess it could be worse. These guys might not be good guys, but they are definitely the lesser of the evils I've had to endure.

"Take a shower, get some rest. I'll have someone bring you food in a bit. You need anything else?" he asks, and I shake my head, no. With that, he closes the door behind me, leaving me in the small room. I stand there for a minute, just taking in the new situation and processing everything that has happened in the last few hours.

I'm tired, so freaking tired, I could fall asleep standing up, but the smell of my armpits is enough to wake the dead, so I definitely need to take a shower first. I start to explore the room, and just like he said, there are men's clothes in the closet and towels in the bathroom. The shower is stocked with new soap and shampoo.

Stripping out of my soiled clothes, I turn the water on hot and take the longest shower of my life. I wash my hair and rinse it three times until I feel clean enough to get out. I felt so dirty after not showering for days.

When I'm done, I dry off and slip into one of the oversized men's T-shirts, and crawl into the bed. It doesn't look like it, but after sleeping on the grimy old mattress, this seems to be the most comfortable thing ever.

It doesn't take me long to fall asleep. I feel myself drifting off the moment my head hits the pillow. My last thought is that I hope tomorrow is going to be a better day.

5

Zane

Matteo wasn't happy when I came back to the house without Dove in hand. In fact, he was almost more upset than me, which confused and enraged me all at once. The beast in me was beating violently against the cage that housed him, wanting so badly to break free. Part of me wanted to unleash him just to see what would happen. Dove is mine, and I'll kill him to prove it if I have to.

All I have to do is hold out a little bit longer before I can kill him and toss him aside, like the asshole he is. Until then, I have to follow his orders, at least if I want to find Dove. Which, as of right now, includes going to Damon Rossi's strip club to demand a meeting with his brother, which I'm one-hundred percent sure isn't going to happen.

"Why do I have to take Alberto with me?"

"Because I said so," Matteo says. I don't understand why he insists on his second in command coming with me to see Damon Rossi. There must be more behind it than him sending a babysitter.

"I don't care to be a part of your pissing contest with Xander Rossi. All I care about is Dove," I barely get the words out. My patience is as thin as the blade I plan to slit Matteo's throat with.

"This is part of getting her back, you want her back, you do this. Otherwise, you might as well have tied a nice little bow around her."

"Shut up!" I growl, knowing that if I didn't need this bastard right now, I would already have bashed his head in.

"I shouldn't have to tell you to be grateful that I'm even offering to help you. I could've shot you dead, after the way you marched in here," he sneers, curling his lip. "Remember, it's you who needs me... I don't need you."

I don't get a chance to respond before he walks out, the sound of the door slamming, echoes through the room. I'm exhausted, angry, and disappointed...I've never felt the way I'm feeling right now. Hopeless beyond measure. I'm doing everything I can to stay afloat, but the waves of despair keep crashing into me. I need Dove. Need her scent surrounding me, need to feel her body against mine, but above all, I just need to know that she is okay, and none of that will happen until I finally have her in my arms again.

Shoving the emotions that are threatening to overtake my psyche down, I mentally prepare myself to talk to Damon Rossi. I'm not stupid, walking in there and demanding a meeting with Xander isn't going to go well for me. The fucker will most likely laugh in my face, but I have to do this. I have to try and find out where they have Dove, and what they're doing to her. This is no longer about her just being mine.

This is about me protecting her, saving her. We were destined to be together since the night she was dropped off at my foster home, and though I'm nobody's white knight, I'll do anything to save her. *Anything.*

～

A NEON SIGN flashes brightly back at me as I pull into the parking lot of *Night Shift.* I've been pissed off since I left Matteo's, and I get the feeling coming here is only going to sour my mood further. I'm tired of the mafia games. I never should've left the safe house with Dove.

I know Donna was dying, and that Dove never would've forgiven me for not being able to say goodbye, but I could deal with her hate if it meant she was safe and sound, tucked into my bed every night beside me. Instead, here we are because I let my feelings for her call the shots, instead of my brain. Sighing, I turn the car off and open the driver's side door.

Climbing out of the car, I stretch my tight muscles before closing the car door. Alberto climbs out of the passenger side and follows me across the parking lot.

Here goes nothing. Maybe if I'm lucky, Damon takes mercy on me. Though that's doubtful. My boots scuff against the concrete as I walk to the front door. It seems like it takes an eternity to get there. Opening the door, I step inside, the place is surprisingly clean, and bigger than I thought it would be, based on the size of the building.

Walking up to the bar with Alberto on my heels like a dog, I'm greeted by a half-dressed woman. She looks to be a little older than Dove, her eyes glitter with excitement when they land on me. The place is mostly deserted, other than a few bar patrons. Looks like I got here before the real show started. Doesn't matter, I didn't come here to watch chicks strip. Pulling my gun out, I set it on the wooden bar, and let her make of it what she will.

She blinks slowly and gives me a grim look. "If you're looking for a fight, you've come to the wrong place. This is a strip club."

Her eyes dart to someone over in the corner of the room, and I know without a doubt, she's calling one of the bouncers over here without even saying a word.

Footsteps sound behind me, and I smirk, my blood pulses in my veins and my muscles tighten, the anticipation of a fight does crazy things to my body.

As soon as his meaty club lands on my arm, I turn on the barstool, grab it, twist it around until I hear a snap, and press it against his chest.

With my other hand, I punch him right in his ugly face, a river of red blood erupts from his nose as he stumbles backward, colliding with a nearby table. I punch him again for safe measure, and because I really want to beat the fuck out of someone. Like a piece of paper, he crumples to the ground.

Out of the corner of my eye, I catch Alberto standing a few feet away, arms crossed over his large chest. He is shaking his head at me like he is disappointed in my undiplomatic behavior. *Well, fuck you.*

"Shit!" The young girl behind the bar mutters under her breath. I turn around to face her once more and find her face ashen, the excitement in her eyes before is replaced with fear. It's a much better look for her. She has no idea the things I'm capable of doing, the things I will do if I don't get the information I want.

"I'm here to speak to Damon Rossi," I growl.

Her gaze widens, and she scurries across the bar and picks up the phone, but she never gets to call whoever it is she'd planned on calling.

"Zane Brennan. I'd say it's a pleasure to meet you, but we both know it's not." Damon Rossi's deep voice meets my ear. Whirling around, I come face to face with the asshole. He briefly turns his attention to my unwanted companion.

"Alberto, didn't expect you to show your face here," he says before pinning me with his gaze once more.

"Where is she? I know you have her here. I went to Christian's compound. She wasn't there, and I know that your brother took her with him when he left the place. I don't have to tell you what will happen if you don't give me the answers I want."

I've got a death wish fucking with the Rossi family, but I might as well be dead if I don't have Dove in my life.

"Who is *she?*" Damon cocks his head to the side like he doesn't know what the hell I'm talking about. His confused expression makes me want to smash his face like a pop can. When it comes to being an asshole, Damon is the worst of the Rossi brothers. Xander might be ruthless and heartless, but Damon is a completely different can of worms. "I don't know who it is that you're referring to."

"You do." I take a threatening step toward him.

Damon looks like a typical mobster with his perfect suit and slicked-back hair. But I know more about him than he thinks. I know he's happily married, and he has a cute little family with 2.5 kids that he would do anything to protect.

"You and your brother have someone who doesn't belong to you, and I want her back, unharmed. Otherwise, I'll be forced to take something pretty and sweet of yours."

The sly grin that was on his face just moments ago has evaporated into the air. In its place is a dark emotionless mask.

"You touch my family, and you'll wish death finds you before I do."

"Then you know how I feel right now. Dove is mine, and I know your brother has her in his possession."

Damon shrugs. "I don't know anything about a girl. But I can tell you that Xander doesn't do meetings unless it's a business deal that benefits him. So, if you don't have something to offer in exchange for this girl—if he even has her—I would get the fuck out of my club while I still have the patience to let you walk out of here."

"Where is she? I want answers!" I'm very close to my breaking point, so close I can almost taste the destruction in the air.

"And I'm telling you, get the fuck out of here before I put a bullet between your eyes." The way he's looking at me, tells me he's not lying, and I'm torn on if I should continue to push him or just walk out. When I see him reaching for his gun, I lunge for him, but fucking Alberto grabs me from behind and pulls me back.

"If you die, you're no use to anyone," Alberto growls. I shrug him off, hating to admit it, but he is right. I'm no good to Dove if I'm dead.

Staring into Damon's eyes, I hope he sees just how badly I want to hurt him. I'm restraining myself, walking a very thin rope of rage. "This isn't over. I'll be back, and when I am, you'll tell me everything I need to fucking know." Damon smirks like he doesn't believe me, and I turn my back to him. On my way out, in a fit of rage, I toss a chair over my shoulder.

I don't care if he shoots me. Let him. Matteo will come for me, eventually, because to him, I'm a pawn in his war against the Rossi's. He needs me just like I need him, even if he won't admit it. Walking back out to the SUV, it takes every ounce of self-restraint I have to continue walking and not turn around.

I want answers, and it feels like I'm giving up on Dove by not getting them. It's only been a few days, but each day that passes without her by my side worries me more. Is she eating? Showering? Are they hurting her? Is she okay?

Fuck. Getting into the car, I drive back to Matteo's mansion. When we arrive, I find the bastard sitting in his study with a glass of whiskey in his hand.

"Have a seat, gentlemen," he says. Alberto takes the seat next to his boss, but all I do is cross my arms over my broad chest and stare him down like a disapproving parent.

"I told you walking in there and demanding to speak to Xander wasn't going to work, and still you sent us. I wanted to kill that asshole so badly it took everything in me not to wipe the floor with his face."

Matteo smirks. "And you're not the first to feel that way about Damon Rossi. He takes some getting used to."

"I don't want to get used to him. I want to find Dove and leave this world behind me."

"Your debt to me isn't paid until I say so, there will be none of that."

Teeth grinding, I tell him, "You've done nothing but make me run around with my head cut off. I don't owe you shit until Dove is safe and secure in my arms."

Swirling the whiskey in his glass, he stares at the amber liquid like it holds all the answers to our problems. As if it would be that easy.

"Damon said Xander won't even consider a meeting unless we have something to offer him." Matteo looks up from the glass, a mischievous glint in his eyes.

"That's not surprising in the least bit. The man is a businessman after all, so I wouldn't expect any different." He pauses. "The best I can offer him is some territory, give him a chance to expand a little."

"You're going to give him land?" I blink, surprised that he's offering anything at all. I was so sure that when I came back here and told him that, he would tell me that this was a lost cause, and I would be forced to go into Rossi territory guns blazing but color me shocked. "Why would you do that?"

"Why do you sound so surprised?" he asks.

I shrug. "Dove isn't your concern, and all I've asked for is your men and some weapons. Yet you offer me more... why?"

Sighing, he places his glass down on the desk. "It's complicated..."

"I have time. There is something you are not telling me, and I need to know what's going on. You know damn well how dangerous it is not knowing a vital piece of information.

"This needs to stay between you and me for now," he says, shooting me a threatening look. When I nod, he continues. "The truth is, Dove is my daughter."

What the fuck did he just say?

"That's why Christian wanted her and why he searched for her for so many years. He most likely planned to use her against me in some way. I mean, that's what I would've done if he had a daughter he was looking for, and I found her first."

"Wait..." I try and comprehend what he's saying. "You're Dove's father?"

He nods. "Yes, her mother and I were in love. She was married, but it was a loveless marriage. When she found out she was pregnant, she was so happy; we both were. She had planned to run away with me. Somewhere along the way, she escaped her husband but never came to me. I thought she was dead, but as I found out later, she had Dove. Then her past caught up with her. Before I could save her, I found out her husband had killed her. Made it look like an overdose, but I know it was him. My daughter was gone by the time I found out. I'd spent years searching for her but always came up empty-handed."

This... it can't be real. Matteo can't be Dove's father. She can't possibly be a part of this fucked up dark world. She's so innocent and sweet. So perfect, and all this world does is take and break you.

"That explains why you want her now, so you can use her," I say, looking down at the floor. I can't believe that after everything, Dove's father is alive, and the leader of one of the biggest mob families. How did this happen? He's just going to hurt her, and I'm going to have to kill him if he does.

"I don't want to use her, Zane. I want a relationship with my daughter. I want her to stand beside me at the throne of the Castro family."

"She doesn't know this life. She's fragile, innocent..." I tell him.

"She is now because she doesn't know any better, but she will get used to it. It's in her blood." We stare at each other for a long moment, and I swear, I can see him moving his chess pieces around, placing them strategically. "Now, we go back to Damon and tell him the offer. She's my daughter, and I'm never leaving her behind again."

Instantly, I know this changes everything... Dove is in more danger than I ever could've imagined, and I'm not sure I can protect her from the evil that's lurking in the dark, murky waters.

6

Dove

When I wake, I feel so rested that I actually forget where I am for a moment. Then reality slams back into me. I open my eyes and stare at the bare ceiling, wondering if I'm ever going to be free again or if I'm just going to be shoved from one prison to the next.

Taking a deep breath, I stretch my arms over my head. I must still be asleep because I swear, I can smell coffee.

Freshly brewed coffee...

"Did you sleep well?" A voice startles me, and I jolt from the bed like the blanket is on fire and scan the room for any threats. My eyes collide with Xander, who is sitting in the corner of the room. He's casually leaning back in the flimsy chair like it's completely normal to watch someone while they're sleeping.

"W-what are you doing here?" I ask when I catch my breath.

"It's my compound, I can go wherever I want, this room included."

"Yeah, but does it have to be my cell?" I say before I can think.

Xander stands up suddenly, and I take a step back, my legs bumping into the side of the bed. I sit down, unsure of what else to do.

"None of this is *yours*. You should be more appreciative of how well I've been treating you. Don't forget, Ivan could have left you there to die."

"I know..." I lower my head. I do know, but that doesn't mean I accept the situation that I'm in.

"Not many people are brave enough to talk to me like that." He walks over to my bed, and I have to crane my neck to look at him. He reaches for something on the nightstand and hands it to me. I look up and find he is extending the cup of coffee out to me.

"Thank you," I whisper, and take the cup from his hand.

"I brought you some clothes. You should be about this size if I figured right." He points to a stack of clothes next to the bed that I hadn't noticed until now.

"Oh..." Is all I can get out at the moment. Over the rim of the cup, I watch him sit back down while I take a sip of the coffee. It's so delicious, I almost moan out loud. Which leads me to my next question. "Why *are* you treating me... this way, like a friend, instead of a foe?"

He has no reason to treat me with kindness. I'm a nobody, and he is some big huge mob boss. It hasn't stopped me from thinking about the fact that he could kill me, use me, or sell me. I'm of value to him in other ways, and yet he brings me clothes and coffee.

"You remind me of someone," he explains. I think he's about to tell me more, tell me who I remind him of, but all he says is, "Zane isn't dead."

I almost drop the cup of coffee into my lap, my clammy hands just barely keep ahold of the mug. Did he just say that?

"Are you sure?" I ask. I want nothing more than to believe him, but I also don't want to get my hopes up just to be crushed again.

"He came to see my brother last night, demanding a meeting with me." Hope blooms in my chest. He's alive, and he's coming to rescue me. "He knows you're here."

"Is... is he coming? Is he coming here?" I try not to sound overly excited, but I'm giddy to see Zane, to wrap my arms around him, to be reunited with him. Never did I think I'd beg to see the man who kidnapped me and kept me hidden from the world, but here I am.

"My brother sent him away last night, he didn't know about you being here. But don't worry. I'm sure Zane will be back soon. He seemed quite determined on getting you back."

"He won't stop. He'll kill all of you. Please, just let me go to him."

"Do you know where Zane is?"

"Oh...well, no." I guess I don't. But... "Zane had security built into my apartment. Cameras and stuff. If you let me go there, maybe he'll see it?"

"You think Christian doesn't have someone watching your apartment? You really don't know anything about our world, do you?" I get the feeling the words are spoken more to himself than to me, but I answer anyway.

"I told you, I don't, and I don't care about Christian. I just want to find Zane."

"I'm not letting you go anywhere, and to be very clear, I don't know if I'll hand you over to Zane at all. Even if he comes for you. There is something about you... I can't put my finger on it. But my gut tells me to keep you here, and my gut is usually right. Maybe you're going to be useful to me later. I don't know yet. For now, drink your coffee and enjoy your stay. You might be here for a while."

And with that, he gets up and walks out of the room, leaving me alone with my suppressed anger and thoughts.

〜

EVEN THOUGH I'M in a cell, I'm treated surprisingly well. A guard brings me food three times a day, which is actually pretty good, no that's a lie. It's delicious. It tastes like it's been prepared by a gourmet chef, which is strange since I'm being held as a captive. I don't know why I'm being treated so well here, but I'm not about to complain over my treatment.

Right after lunch, two days after arriving here, I hear someone talking on the other side of my door. Moments later, the door unlocks and swings open. Sinking down onto the edge of the mattress, I'm not sure what to expect, but it wasn't the tiny woman I'm greeted by. She enters my cell slowly, almost as if she's worried someone is going to see her.

"Hi... you must be, Dove," she whispers, a soft smile creeping onto her face. Her blonde hair is long and cascades down her back in gentle waves. She looks like an angel, pure, soft, and kind.

"Um, hi," I say awkwardly. "Yes, I'm Dove."

"I'm Ella, Xander's wife."

Xander's wife? He's married? I guess I never considered him to be the marrying type.

"Oh, ah... thanks for loaning me the clothes. You can have them back... uhhh, whenever I get to leave."

"No problem, don't worry about it. You can keep them if you like. Xander likes to spoil me. I've got more clothes than I could wear in this lifetime." Her laugh is carefree, and I can't help but feel jealous.

Not of her clothes but of her having Xander and embracing it. I was so stupid. I had it all, and I threw it all away. I fought Zane tooth and nail, instead of just enjoying the time we had together.

"Do you mind if I sit?" Ella asks, pointing to the spot beside me on the bed.

"No, please do."

She smiles and takes the seat next to me. "I'm sorry they're holding you here. I know it sucks getting caught in the middle of something that's not your fault. I thought I could at least come by and check on you, give you some company, so you're not so alone all day."

Her genuineness is almost too much. I have no clue why she is being so nice to me, but being deprived of human contact for the most part, over the last few days, has me really appreciating the gesture.

"Thank you," I say, having the odd urge to hug her as well. Since that would be a little weird, I refrain. Unable to think of anything else to ask, I blurt out, "So, how did you and Xander meet?"

She scoots up on the bed, leaning her back against the wall like she is getting comfortable.

Is she going to stay here with me?

"Believe it or not, it was a very similar situation to the way you met him. I was being held captive by his father. He was a bad man, and he was about to hurt me... Xander and his men raided the compound I was being held at. He saved me and took me home."

Now his comment about me reminding him of someone makes sense. He must have meant his wife since we were in a similar situation.

"Wow... and you just stayed here with him? Did he not give you the chance to leave?"

"I didn't want to leave." Ella smiles. "But, don't worry, he won't keep you here forever."

"Are you sure about that?"

"He has no reason to." Ella shrugs. "He's just keeping you right now until he finds the best way to..." She trails off, unable to find the right word.

"The best way to use me?" I finish for her. "I mean, you don't have to sugarcoat it. He is using me as a bargaining chip to get what he wants, isn't he?"

Ella lowers her head in shame. "I'm sorry, but yes. Yes, he is."

"Don't be sorry, it's not your fault. I just wish I could talk to Zane."

"Who is Zane?" Ella asks curiously.

"He is my... well, I don't really know what he is." *My everything.*

I spend the next ten minutes telling Ella my story. I tell her how Zane and I met in foster care and that I thought he died. We talk about him kidnapping me, and then me getting kidnapped again by Christian.

"So, what else do you do? Besides getting kidnapped on a regular basis?" Ella chuckles, and I can't help but giggle with her. For the first time in many days, I laugh, actually laugh.

We talk for a while, Ella tells me about her sister being married to Ivan and how they were pregnant at the same time. Momentarily, I forget where I am and why I'm here. Right now, it feels like it's just an old friend and me catching up.

Reality comes crashing back down on me when I hear an angry voice yelling at the guard in front of my door. A few seconds later, the door swings open, and Xander waltzes inside, wearing a mask of fury on his face.

"What the hell are you doing here?" He scowls at Ella, who seems completely unaffected by his stare. A stare that has a shiver running down my spine.

"Don't overreact. I'm fine. We were just talking." She gets up and goes to stand by his side, touching his arm tenderly. I can see the rage seeping away from his body, from across the room. His shoulders relax, and the white-knuckled fists by his sides, turn back to lax hands.

"Go back home, mouse," he tells her. She pushes up onto her tiptoes and gives him a chased kiss on the lips before heading out of the room, but not before giving me a tiny wave goodbye. As soon as she's gone, I miss her presence. It's like she's taken the warmth in the room with her.

"Put your shoes on, it's time to go," Xander orders, crossing his arms in front of him.

The news leaves me shocked. "What do you mean? Where am I going?"

"Zane and Matteo arranged a meeting with me. They want to trade you for some territory."

I should probably be offended that I'm being bargained with for a plot of land, but right this second, all I can process is that I'm finally going to get to see Zane again. I jump up from the bed and put my shoes on in a hurry.

"Why is Matteo willing to give up land for you?"

"Who?" I ask as I straighten up. "Who is Matteo?"

"One of my rivals as well as Christian's. Zane must have some valuable information he is trading... or something else? What if he has information that can hurt me in the long run?"

For a moment, I think he is going to change his mind. I can see him thinking about it, weighing his options.

"Look, Xander, you treated me well, and like you said, you did save me from Christian. I owe you, if you bring me to Zane and I find something out that could harm you or your family, I will tell you. I swear."

Xander examines me for a long minute. Just when I think he is going to lock me back in here, he disappears into the hallway but leaves the door open for me. Relief washes over me. He is still letting me go.

Hesitantly, I step outside. There are still two guards outside the door, and all three men resemble that of bouncers at a club, tall and muscular, making me feel even smaller than I am.

Looking up at the men, neither of them make eye contact with me. Without a word, Xander starts walking, the two men flanking him. I fall into step and follow them down the hall. When we get to the entrance, I find more men waiting at the door, and even more outside. All dressed in black, weapons attached to their hips, looking like an army about to take down a city.

"Everyone knows their orders, so let's go," Xander calls out, his voice void of emotion. There are four blacked-out SUVs parked in front of the building, and at Xander's word, the men start piling into them. I stare, trying to figure out where I fit in in all of this. Do I just go to one of the SUV's and get in? As if Xander can sense my confusion, his dark gaze turns to me.

"You're coming with me," he says.

Before I can take a step, Xander's hand circles my upper arm, and he starts pulling me toward one of the cars. Excitement and anxiety over the unknown swirls deep in my gut. What's going to happen next? Am I really going to be reunited with Zane, or is this a joke?

Xander opens the back door to one of the SUV's and shoves me inside. I'm surprised to find someone already sitting in the back seat. The moment his eyes meet mine, I have this odd sense of deja vu. This man looks at me the same way Xander looked at me the first time we met. On top of that, he resembles Xander, almost to a tee. Like they could totally be—

"This is Damon, my brother," Xander says before I can finish my thought.

Forced into the middle seat, I place my hands in my lap. Xander slides in next to me, sandwiching me between him and his brother.

The car starts, and before I know it, we are driving away from the building and off the compound. An eerie silence settles over us, and I don't know where to look. The two men sitting in the front? The two men sitting on either side of me? Or just straight ahead on the road before us? Yes, I'll go with the road. It's the safer bet.

With my hands in my lap, I squeeze my shoulders together, trying to make myself as small as possible. When my eyes wander, and I look out to the side window, I catch Damon's eyes on me. Even when he sees me looking, he keeps staring at me, and I don't know how to feel about that. It's like he doesn't care that I caught him watching me, which intensifies the anxiousness that I'm already feeling.

"Xander tells me you're twenty-one?" Damon finally breaks the silence. His voice is just as dark and ominous as his brother's.

"Yes." I nod my head, not understanding why my age is being brought up, yet again.

"We're almost there," Xander announces. "Lean forward."

"Huh?" I twist around to look at him, but he is already pushing on my shoulders, forcing me to lean forward.

"Put your hands behind your back," he orders while digging for something in his pocket. My eyes catch on a pair of cable ties, only then, do I realize what he is up to.

"I won't run..."

"That's not the point. Just do it," he growls, and I slowly bring my hands to the small of my back. Every inch of my body is shaking. I'm not sure if I'm scared of him, or of what's going to happen next. Xander grips my arms and fastens the cable ties around my wrists to the point of pain. The plastic cuts into my skin, but I don't complain.

With my hands tied behind my back, I awkwardly and uncomfortably lean back against the seat. Neither of the Rossi brothers says anything to me, and once again, the car is blanketed in silence. We drive a few more minutes before pulling up to a large parking lot behind an abandoned warehouse. *Oh no... I've seen movies.*

I know the kind of shady shit that happens at abandoned warehouses, and it's nothing good. We circle the building like sharks, and I catch sight of another fleet of vehicles.

That must be Zane.

My heart starts beating faster and my throat swells. Am I really going to see him? What am I going to say? What is he going to say? Will he be mad at me? I never thought this would actually happen, so I never prepared myself for the scenario.

All my internal questions are cut off when I feel a hand on top of my head. Before I can turn to see who is touching me, the hand ruffles through my hair. Like a ten-year-old boy would do to a girl to make her mad.

"Hey! What the hell?" I whine, trying to move away from the hand.

"Can't have you looking all put together and shit. You were my prisoner after all," Xander explains. When he is done making a knotty mess of my hair, he takes the fabric of my shirt and rips it around my shoulder and down my arm. "There you go. That's better."

I look over at him, dumbfoundedly. "So, if they ask about where you kept me, should I lie? Maybe make up some dungeon?"

Xander smirks. "Smart girl, you are, though there isn't any need to make it up. There is a dungeon at my place, and as far as everybody knows, that's where you were kept."

"Got it." I nod, just as the car is put into park.

The front doors open first, the guards climb out and open the back doors. Damon is the first out. When I scoot toward his door to slip out, Xander grabs me by the arm, tugging me toward his door instead.

Sliding across the seat, he pulls me out of the car. My feet land against the concrete, and I suck in a precious breath of oxygen, almost as if I hadn't been breathing the entire drive here.

Xander doesn't give me a chance to prepare myself and starts walking toward the caravan of vehicles. Good thing he has an iron grip on my arm because the first step I take, I trip and almost faceplant. Xander pulls me up, and I fall in step beside him.

As soon as I lift up my head, I spot Zane and another man, off in the distance. My entire body locks up and my heart tightens in my chest.

He's really alive.

Our eyes connect, and even from a distance, I can see the turmoil of emotions in their depths, relief, need, and overwhelming possessiveness. Zane is mine, and I am his. I realize that now. My feet move of their own accord. My body drawn to him like a magnet. I try to run toward him, wanting to tell him that I'm okay. That everything is going to be okay. But Xander jerks me back by the arm, keeping me close to his side before I can take off.

Zane's eyes lower to where Xander's hand is. His lip curls almost as if he is snarling like an animal. The glare in his eyes is deadly, and I'm positive that it's taking every ounce of self-restraint he has, not to charge at Xander right now. The mere thought of a fight breaking out between the two of them is terrifying.

I can feel Zane's rage rolling off of him in waves. I don't know how this meeting is going to end. I just hope that after everything we've been through, that Zane and I can walk away in one piece.

7

Zane

I'm a bullet waiting to leave the chamber. My body vibrates with unchecked rage. Every fiber and cell in my body is telling me to move. Telling me to go to her, and rip Xander Rossi's hand off of her body and beat him with it for touching her. For touching what is mine and always will be mine.

Like a ticking time bomb, I force myself to stand still, to hold back. I know it's the most strategic thing to do, but that doesn't make it any easier. If he does something stupid, or if I see Dove flinch even once, I'll explode. I didn't come all this way not to leave with her, but I won't let him or anyone else hurt her.

"It's a pleasure to finally meet you, Zane." Xander's lips tip up at the sides in a smile when we're just a few feet away. "Matteo, it's been a while. I would say it's good to see you, but we both know that's a lie. If it wasn't for this agreement, I'd have my men pumping you full of lead by now."

"Same." Matteo nods, and all I can think is how fucked up these two fuckers are. I need to get Dove and get us out of here before these two end up firing their guns in some sick fight to see whose cock is bigger.

Damon, Xander's brother, is watching me. I can feel his beady eyes on my skin, burning through my flesh. "The agreement has been signed by both parties and is final. You can have the girl back. We had our fun with her. I'm pretty sure she enjoyed her stay as well."

Xander fully grins, and I clench my fist, envisioning my hand wrapping around his throat and squeezing. If he touched her, I will kill him. I'll rip him to pieces, no matter what war I'll start in doing soon. I'd kill anyone, bloody my hands in any way to protect her.

"Let her go," I say through clenched teeth, surprised that the words don't come out as an animalistic growl.

"Hand over the papers first," Xander orders like I'm one of his men. Matteo nods to Karl, one of his guys, and he starts walking toward the space between our two groups. Damon takes a few steps forward, meeting Karl and snatches the papers from him.

He looks over them quickly before motioning to Xander that it's all good. Instead of letting Dove go right away, which would be the smart thing to do, Xander pulls her closer to him, leans down, and whispers something into the shell of her ear.

That's it. He's going to die...

Taking a step forward, I'm fully prepared to wrap my hands around the fucker's neck when Matteo and one of his goons, grab me by the arms, holding me back. I shrug them off, giving both of them a look that says don't fucking touch me.

When I turn my attention back to Xander and Dove, he lets her go.

As soon as he releases her, she runs toward me, almost losing her balance with her hands tied behind her back. A moment later, her slim body slams into mine. She buries her face in my chest, and I wrap my arms around her protectively. Before I do anything, I bury my face into the crook of her neck and inhale deeply. This moment is like seeing the sun after a long cold winter. Like tasting water after a drought. It's indescribable but all the words at once.

"I missed you so much," she mumbles into my chest. "I thought you were dead."

"I missed you too," I reply, stroking a hand down her back. I want to strip her bare, look her over, and worship every inch of her body. I want to ask her what happened, if she's okay, if she is hungry, tired, or hurt, but I also just want to stand here like this, doing nothing more than holding her.

"Let's go," Matteo says, nudging me in the side. I'm tempted to tell him to fuck off, but I bite my tongue. Getting Dove away from these guys is what I need to do. Now that I have her back in my arms, protecting her and ensuring her safety is my number one priority. Nothing in this world will ever separate us again.

Matteo offers me his knife, and I take it, cutting the plastic zip ties binding her wrists. As soon as her hands are free, she wraps her arms around me. There is nothing like feeling her tiny arms wrapped around me. It's so strange that once upon a time, she tried to escape me, but now she holds me close as if I'm her savior.

I lean down and whisper into her ear. "I want nothing more than to hold you in my arms, but we really need to go."

Nodding, she pulls away, her beautiful blue eyes are filled with tears, making them seem lighter. "I'm sorry, Zane. I'm sorry I didn't listen to you. That I made you take me to the hospital. It's all my fault." Big fat tears fall from her eyes, and my heart cracks a little in my chest.

"It's okay, baby, and it's not your fault. We'll talk when we get back to Matteo's place," I tell her.

Wrapping an arm around her shoulders, I turn and guide us back to the SUV. Matteo's men swarm us like we're the president of the United States, which for once, I'm actually grateful for. When we reach the car, I open the door and lift her inside before climbing in myself. Pulling her tight to my side, I press my lips to her forehead.

This feels like a dream. And I'm waiting for the other shoe to drop. Like at any second, I'm going to wake up and realize that none of it was real. That I imagined the whole thing, and that Dove isn't really here with me.

Matteo climbs into the front seat, and one of his men takes the driver's seat. Even as the car starts to move, it still doesn't feel real.

"Where are we going?" Dove whispers, peering up at me through her wet lashes.

"Matteo's place. I have so much to tell you... but first, I need to make sure you're okay. Did they hurt you? Touch you in any way?" Bile rises in my throat as I speak. God, I don't know if I can handle this. If either of them fuckers touched her...I'll lose it. Fury overtakes every emotion I'm feeling at the moment.

"Neither of them hurt me, and I wasn't with Christian long before Xander's men found me."

Thank fuck... I was getting ready to paint the entire world red.

Sighing, I hold onto her a little tighter. "All I could think about the entire time they had you was if you were okay. If they were hurting you? If you were eating, or if you were cold? All I could think about was saving you and how I had let you down."

"No," Dove whimpers and grips onto my shirt as if I'll disappear at any second. I'm certain she is close to shattering, and things are only going to get worse from here. "It's not your fault, none of this is your fault, Zane. You tried to protect me. You warned me, and I wouldn't listen. I thought you were crazy, but if I had believed you—"

"Don't worry about that right now..."

"Hate to break up your reunion, but I believe you owe me a thank you," Matteo announces from the front seat.

Rolling my eyes, I grit my teeth as I speak my next set of words. "Thank you, Matteo." Playing nice with this guy is trying on my patience, and I'm not sure how much longer I can go before I snap and do something drastic.

"That doesn't sound like you're really grateful, but I'll let it slide since you've finally delivered on bringing my daughter back to me."

Fucking Christ. Why did he have to go and say that? I was hoping to spill the beans to Dove once we were back at the house.

"Wha-what is he talking about, Zane?" Dove blinks, but the shocked expression on her face doesn't dissipate.

Tension fills the vehicle. "Dammit, I didn't want to do this yet, Matteo."

"Why not?" He shifts in his seat. "There is no better time than the present to let my daughter know that her father isn't dead and didn't abandon her."

"You're my father?" Dove whispers so quietly I almost don't hear her. "How... how is that possible?" She looks from me and back to Matteo, and I wish, now more than ever, that I had told her no when she begged me to go see Donna one last time. Maybe if I had said no, none of this would've happened.

Matteo snickers. "Well, I'm sure I don't have to tell you where babies come from, so I'll skip that part, but you see, your mother was actually a married woman who happened to fall in love with me. When she found out she was pregnant, we had planned to run away together. However, she had a change of heart and disappeared. When I finally found her, she was dead, and you were gone. I looked everywhere for you, but every trail led me to a dead-end. I was sure I would never find you, and then Zane came to me. As soon as he told me that Christian had been looking for you for many years, I knew who you were."

Just from the way she tenses beside me, I can tell Dove isn't just shocked but uncomfortable as well.

Turning toward me as if I can shield her from the truth, she opens her mouth and asks me the one question I know will be the final nail in her coffin. "Is it true? Is he really my father?"

My throat tightens, and as badly as I want to lie, I know it won't change anything. It won't help her. Finding out Matteo is her father, was a surprise. I thought I could get help and slip away into the night with Dove, but now I know that's not possible. Matteo is going to do whatever he can to keep Dove in his life, and I'll be fighting a war I can't win if I try and keep her from him.

"Yes, he's your father," I say.

All I can do is watch with an ache in my chest as she works through the emotions, agony, fear, and confusion flicker across her beautiful features. After watching her closely for years, I can almost tell how she's going to react to a situation before she even does. It's weird, but an added plus to having stalked her for years.

"I know it's a lot to take in on such short notice, especially after everything that's happened, but I want you to know that now that I've found you, I plan to get to know you better, and be the father I never got to be," Matteo says.

Father? I choke back my laughter. I haven't known him long, but Matteo doesn't take me as the father type. He's the leader of the Castro family. All he knows how to do is order his men around and threaten people. Plus, what kind of parenting is he going to do? Dove's an adult now and doesn't need his money or protection. Not when she has me.

Dove is quiet the rest of the way back to the house, and when we arrive at the mansion, she seems a little overwhelmed. Once out of the car and inside the house, I take Dove's hand into mine. "Thank you so much for helping me find her, but I think it's time we end this charade. Her safety is my biggest priority."

Matteo stares at me, his face blank. Two of his men hover just outside the massive wooden front door. I can feel their eyes on me.

"There is no safer place for her than here, surely, you can agree, given that you were the one to put her in the situation that got her taken by Christian in the first place?"

His remark is a kick to the balls, and if it wasn't for Dove standing beside me, I'd have him pinned to the wall. Strangling the air from his lungs. Still, fighting with him on staying for the night isn't something I want to do. Not when I could be holding Dove in my arms, kissing every inch of her skin, and making up for lost time.

"Fine, we will stay for tonight," I say, pinning him with a glare.

"Great, why don't you go upstairs and get some rest? Karl will take you up." He smiles, his eyes twinkling with some unknown emotion.

I don't bother paying him another second of attention. Shifting gears, I tug Dove toward the grand staircase. Karl follows behind all the way to our room, like the guard dog he is.

Opening the door, I guide us into the room. The door shuts with a soft click, and all I can think is... *finally*, finally, we're alone.

"Do we really have to stay here? This is wrong. Something feels off." Concern is etched into her delicate face.

"Only for tonight. Tomorrow we will figure this out. Everything can wait until then because the only thing that matters to me right now is making sure you're okay and reminding you of how much you mean to me."

"I thought I lost you," Dove says. Her voice is clogged with emotion.

"You'll never lose me," I tell her, pulling her into my arms. I squeeze her tight, wanting to melt our two bodies into one.

"Why didn't you tell me?"

"Tell you what?"

"That you are William..."

I peel her away from my chest just enough so I can look at her face. "You remember?"

"Yes. How could I forget you?"

"You told the therapist that you didn't remember that time. She even said it was normal, considering what you've been through. Your mind is trying to protect you and all that shit."

"I told everyone I didn't remember because I never wanted to talk about it. Losing you hurt so bad. Saying it out loud just made it worse."

"Oh, baby." I pull her back into my embrace. "If I had known you'd remembered, I would have told you. That would have made things a whole lot easier."

For a long moment, we just stand there holding each other. Then Dove breaks the silence, whispering, "You came for me..."

"Of course." Does she doubt I would have? She should know the extent of my obsession by now. "No matter what happens, I'll always come for you. I'll always protect you. I'll move heaven and hell to make sure you're safe. You're my number one and always have been. Nothing will ever change that. I love you, Dove. Always..."

8

Dove

His words hit me like a freight train. I'm overcome with emotion. Drowning in it. I'm uncertain about nearly everything at this point, everything but Zane.

I need him. Need to feel his hands on me, to press my lips against his, to carve out a piece of my heart and give it to him. It hasn't been that long since I last saw him, but it feels like years after everything that's happened. Pushing at his chest, I make him walk backward toward the large bed. I want to lie down and curl up on top of his chest.

"Can we please just go to bed? I'm so tired."

"Whatever you want or need, we can do it."

I nod, finally feeling free, safe, and secure. I haven't felt even a sliver of safety since we left the hospital that day.

Zane starts peeling off my clothes until I'm in nothing but a pair of panties. His eyes roaming over my body as if he is inspecting every inch of it.

"No one touched you?" he asks again as if he didn't hear or believe me when I told him earlier.

"No. I promise, I'm fine." I tug on his shirt, wanting his skin to touch mine. He raises his arms, and I help him out of his shirt.

I gasp when I see the fresh bullet wounds. "You were shot!" Three times?" I knew he had been hurt, but nothing prepared me for seeing the wounds up close.

Zane chuckles. "I'm fine, Dove. I'm not that easy to kill."

"I know, but you almost died." Staring at his chest, I can't bring myself to look him in the eyes. I feel immense guilt for those three wounds. Almost as if I was the one that pulled the trigger. Had I not begged to go and see Donna...

Zane's gentle voice cuts off my train of thought, and two fingers lift my chin, forcing me to look into his eyes. "*Almost* isn't the same as did. There was no way in hell I was going to die in that parking garage, knowing that Christian had you. I was put on this earth to protect you, and I don't care if I have to die to do that, Dove. In my eyes, you're the only thing that has ever mattered." The look he's giving me right now says he's telling the truth.

"I'm sorry I didn't believe you. Sorry that I tried to escape, and tried to hurt you..."

"You were only trying to protect yourself." Zane moves his hand, his knuckles grazing against my cheek while tucking some loose strands of hair behind my ear. "I don't blame you, and that's why I never really punished or tried to hurt you. All I wanted to do was keep you safe."

The agony that coats each word reminds me that he, too, feels as if he let me down. Jesus, we're a mess.

My head starts to throb, a migraine from hell, no doubt forming there.

"We have so much to talk about, but all I want to do is crawl into bed and sleep for days."

Zane smirks, his gaze darkening as he drops his hand from my cheek. "I can think of a couple other things we can do besides sleep or talk."

Even though it's probably messed up, that's all I want right now. To be close to Zane, to solidify what we were building before everything exploded in our faces.

Reaching for his already hard cock between our bodies, I look up at him. "I want you. Inside of me. Our bodies skin to skin. I need this. Need to feel every inch of your body blanketing mine."

"Me too, baby, me too."

And that's all he says before he guides me back to the bed. My knees hit the edge of the mattress, and I fall onto my back. Zane crawls up over my body with a predatory glint in his eyes, causing me to shiver, and my nipples harden.

All my worries and fears evaporate in an instant. All that matters is Zane and me. Our bodies and hearts, becoming one.

Like fire and gasoline, we come together, igniting a fiery passion that burns hotter than the sun. Zane peppers every inch of my flesh with hot open mouth kisses, his tongue gliding over my flesh, making the muscles between my thighs clench.

"I can't even put into words how much I missed you." He kisses a path across my collarbone and down between my breasts. Lifting my hips, I try and draw him closer to the place that is aching, pulsing like it has its own heartbeat. "How afraid I was that something bad was happening to you. Since that night that you saved me, I vowed to protect you. I watched you, snuck in your apartment, killed assholes that only wanted you for sex, and guess what?"

He pulls his mouth away, but his tongue still flicks out against my diamond hard nipple, teasing me, tempting me.

"What?" I ask breathlessly, my chest heaving.

A devilish grin tugs at his lips. "I'd do it all again. Over a hundred times. Again, and again because you're mine, Dove. All mine, and the next time someone tries to take you away from me, I won't fail you. I'll kill them with my bare hands, and make you watch just to prove to you that I will never let you down again."

I nod my head, letting him know that I know and that I understand. He rewards me by sucking my nipple into his mouth, tugging on the tip hard until my back is arching off the bed, and I'm holding his head against my breast.

A ravenous need that only he can satiate tightens, swirling

around inside of me, and I have to have him; need him with a desperation that is way too embarrassing to say out loud.

Releasing my nipple with a pop that reverberates through the room, he takes a step back and reaches for my hips. His fingers run along the edge of my cotton panties, and I'm half tempted to shove them down my legs and pull him forward, forcing him to take me, but I know patience is a virtue, and Zane needs this almost more than I do.

"Has anyone touched *my* pussy?"

"No," I croak.

"Are you lying to me?" Zane cocks his head to the side as he slowly tugs the panties down my legs before tossing them over his shoulder. The cool air kisses my wet folds, and I let out a hiss at the sensation.

"No... no one has touched me. I'm yours, only yours..." I'm panting like a dog in heat. I bite my lip, watching through heavy lids as he spreads my legs, his eyes going straight to my soaked core.

"Fuck, Dove. I've missed this pretty little pussy. I've only taken you twice, but I want to bury myself balls deep inside of you and live there forever."

"Yes, please..." My core clenches in response, and I'm so turned on, so ready for him. I need him to take me right now. Take me and own me.

Zane smiles and glides his knuckles against the inside of my thigh as he trails a hand closer to my center. *Yes!*

When his fingers flutter against my swollen folds, I whimper. "You want my fat cock in there. Deep inside you, don't you?"

"Yes, now, please..." I beg helplessly.

"Good because I need you, too, right now. I need you, my Dove, and I need you hard and fast, my balls slapping against your ass, my cock pressing against the back of your channel, giving you both pleasure and pain."

"Yes, Zane. God, please, I need this." Reaching for him, my hand circles his length, and for one brief second, I forgot how large he is. How thick it is, and how full I'm going to be when he enters me.

"You'll get me..." He hisses out through clenched teeth as I squeeze his length and move my hand up and down his shaft.

A gasp escapes my lips, and I tip my head back into the pillows when he enters me with two fingers without warning. I'm so turned on and wet that the intrusion does nothing but fan the flames of arousal. He pumps in and out of me, and stars appear before my eyes.

"Fuck me. I've thought about this moment every night you were gone. Me finding you, saving you, and then worshiping your body, taking every hole over and over again. Your tight little pussy likes that, wants it. She's clenching all around me, do you hear the wet sounds she's making? Do you feel your arousal against your thighs?"

"Yes!" I tug on his cock a little hard, and his thrusts become harder, the heel of his hand presses against my clit, and the added pressure sends me skyrocketing into orgasmic lands. Shivering, my muscles tense and then snap. I clench tightly around Zane's fingers and let out a deranged whimper at the loss of them as he pulls out of me.

I'm seconds away from asking him what he's doing when his body blankets mine, and he grabs my hands and pins them above my head. *Control. Zane is all about control.* With one hand, he holds both my wrists in place, and with the other, he guides his throbbing cock to my entrance.

"Tell me you don't want this, that you don't want me, and I'll take you anyway. I'll still claim your body just as you've claimed my heart, without a single fuck given. You're mine, Dove, mine and only ever mine."

Parting my lips, a response is on the tip of my tongue, but I never say it. All that comes out is a bunch of incoherent thoughts, and pants, and begging for Zane to take me harder and faster as he enters me so deeply all I feel is him, his cock impaling me, owning me.

"Heaven, home, life. Fuck, I didn't know I wasn't breathing until I met you, Dove." Zane bows his head as his grasp on my wrist tightens. He drives into me, rutting, going as deep as he can. My body tingles, goosebumps pebble my flesh, and my nipples rub against his chiseled chest with every stroke, heightening my pleasure.

"Zane... I want..." I can barely get the words out...my thoughts are being overrun by pleasure, by pain.

"What, baby, what do you want?" Zane growls, a bead of sweat dripping down his temple.

"Touch... I want to touch you."

"Your touch makes me insane," he grunts but releases his hold on my hands. As soon as my hands are free, they're on him. He hisses at my touch and thrusts faster, his balls slapping against my ass furiously. His thirst for me is unquenchable, and I'm not sure if he'll ever be able to get enough of me.

Circling my hands around his neck, I pull him closer until his face is buried in my neck, and all I hear are his heavy breaths filling my ears. Kissing along his shoulder, I grip onto him for dear life as he fucks me like a beast. This is nothing like our first or even second time. There is something so raw and beautiful about the way he comes apart. The man who would paint the world red for me becomes melted butter in my hands, and I love it.

With the quickening pace, I find I'm sprinting to the finish line. Lifting my hips, I meet him thrust for thrust. We're two crazed lovers clawing at one another's hearts until they're a bloody mess. Who will bleed the most?

Swiveling his hips, Zane makes it impossible for me to think, or form any coherent thought as the tip of his cock grazes a spot so pleasurable inside of me, I nearly come undone in a second.

"I need you to come. I need to feel you tighten around me, to have you suck the come right out of my cock...will you do that for me?"

I don't know how he's still able to talk. Every nerve ending on my body is electrified, and like sticking a fork into a light socket, the pleasure zings through me, making my toes curl and my back arch off the bed. The gates of pleasure open, and suddenly I'm suffocating, drowning, and damn, would it be the perfect way to go.

"Oh fuck..." Zane growls, wrapping his arms around my back, holding me close to him as he continues to thrust into me while my body tries to push him out. A few more thrusts and he meets his own wave of pleasure, exploding deep inside of me, painting the walls of my womb with his sticky release.

Zane collapses against me, his arms still wrapped around mine. Our chests heave as we try and catch our breaths. Our hearts beat in sync, threatening to come out of our chests.

Sweat covers our bodies, and as the intense orgasm dissipates, everything I pushed to the back of my mind comes barreling to the front. Closing my eyes, I try and push the thoughts away.

Please, not today... I just need one day.

After a while, Zane rolls off of me. He nuzzles his nose against mine and presses a kiss to my forehead so gently I almost don't feel it. It's a stark reminder of how different he can be. How the same hands that bring death to many, also bring me immense pleasure.

"I know the last thing you want right now is to talk about the elephant in the room, but there isn't any way around this. We need to talk about Matteo being your father, and about how we are going to get out of here."

Forcing my heavy eyes open, I find that Zane is sitting on the edge of the bed, his eyes roaming over my body. There is a frantic look hidden in those depths, almost as if he thinks I'm going to disappear on him again.

"How did you get him to help you?"

"Let's just say, I'm indebted to the Castro family for a little while."

Frowning, I reach for his hand and interlace our fingers. "What do you mean, *indebted*?"

Zane's lip curls in disgust, but I know his anger and feelings aren't directed at me. "It means I do as your new-found father says until otherwise."

His response is like a slap in the face back to reality. Yes, Zane wouldn't have been able to get to me without Matteo's help, I realize that, but the last thing I want is for him to be stuck in this world, for both of us to be stuck here. I don't want to be a pawn to anyone, and I want even less for Zane to be.

Shaking my head, I try to process all the information I've learned about today. I have so many questions, so many things I need to know, but my brain is exhausted. All of this has been so tiring...finding out Matteo is my father. I don't know him.

The only thing I'm sure of when it comes to him is that he's evil. The aura he gives off tells me so. I doubt there is a merciful bone in his body. I remember what Xander whispered in my ear before he let me go.

"Don't trust Matteo."

Even without Xander's warning, I wouldn't trust him. It's just another confirmation for me not to do so. I'll be the first to admit, I'm naive to the dark world I've been thrust into, but I'm not stupid. A man like Matteo, like Xander, they're willing to step on anyone that gets in their way, and that includes me. Just because Xander didn't treat me like a true captive, doesn't mean the next time we cross paths, he won't draw blood.

My thoughts swirl and shift, and the sedated feeling I had just a short while ago is gone. In its place, anxiety has bloomed, festering like a wound that won't heal.

"I don't understand..." I whisper more to myself than Zane. "I've been in the system since, well, as long as I can remember. If he was really my father, how did he not find me? Especially since he obviously has money at his disposal."

"As far as I know, both him and Christian have been looking for you for at least a decade, if not longer. Your mom changed her name, and when she died, no one knew who you were or who your father was. You were a Jane Doe for a while, being passed around from foster home to foster home. Then someone decided to give you a name. I don't know everything, but I do know that whatever Matteo is up to is bad. I have to get you away from him."

"Xander said the same thing..."

"What do you mean, Xander said the same thing?" Zane's expression becomes intuitive.

"Xander told me not to trust Matteo. Which I mean, coming from another mobster family doesn't really mean much of anything, but given that he could've hurt me while I was being held captive and he didn't, kind of speaks volumes to me."

My eyes catch on the tightness of Zane's jaw. "They're both criminals, who would kill you the second you became useless to them."

"Are you saying you don't trust Xander?"

"Fuck, no. Why do you trust him?" The defensive tone he's giving me makes it hard for me to want to answer him honestly.

"I don't... I guess... Maybe a little." I shrug. "I mean, he didn't have to treat me the way he did. The room he kept me in was clean and quiet, and none of his men messed with me. He brought me clothes and made sure I was fed well. Although, I'm not supposed to tell anyone any of those things. Plus, I really liked his wife."

"You met his wife?" Zane looks at me like I've grown a second head.

"Yeah, she came and hung out with me. Kept me company, so I wasn't so alone."

For a moment, it seems I've rendered Zane speechless. He just looks at me with wide eyes, his expression flat.

"Wow...I'm kinda shocked. Don't get me wrong. I'm glad he treated you well, but nothing you said is something Xander would do. I wouldn't be surprised if he did this by design. Trying to keep you on his good side for some reason, but that would mean he knew who you were. Which puts you in danger and on his radar."

"Ugh, I don't know. All of this is too much. My brain needs a rest. All I know is that I don't want anything to do with Matteo, even if he is my father. I don't know him, and I don't want to get to know him either."

"And you shouldn't. Matteo might be your father, but I don't think that means much to a man like him, especially when he just found you. I don't know what he has planned, but I won't let him hurt you. Someone like him always has an agenda, and no matter what he says, you're not safe here."

Hearing him say exactly what I've been thinking this whole time, only solidifies what we need to do. We have to escape, but how if Zane is stuck under my new-found father's thumb?

Sitting up, I move a little closer to him. I can feel his come dripping out of me and onto my thighs with the movement. Gripping him by the jaw, I gently turn his face to mine. "I'm not leaving without you, Zane."

His dark gaze looks like it's a million miles away when it finally meets mine. "I was afraid you'd say that..."

9

Zane

By the time morning comes, I'm in no better mood than I was when I went to sleep. The only thing I have to smile about is the fact that I have Dove in my arms when I wake up. Aside from that, I hate this place, and I hate that I'm stuck working for Matteo.

An insistent knock echoes against the wooden door.

"Tell it to go away," Dove grumbles into my chest.

"I wish I could," I reply and roll out of bed. I'm in nothing but my boxers, but I don't care. I'd open the door if I was buck ass naked.

The knocking continues even as I walk to the door. Fondly, I remember a time when I killed men for lesser things. My hands itch to do some damage to whoever is on the other side of that door. Then again, the fact that I have Dove back should give me even more of an incentive not to do something stupid. Killing one of Matteo's men or him would start a full-on war, and without anyone on my side, I'd be as good as dead, and so would Dove.

As soon as I open the door, I want to close it.

"Good morning. Matteo is requesting you have breakfast with him," Karl sneers from just outside the doorway, his beady eyes try and see into the room, but I use my body as a shield to block him.

"Tell him we'll be right down," I say before slamming the door in his face.

When I turn around, Dove is climbing out of bed, completely naked, and heading toward the bathroom. "I'm taking a shower first."

"I'll join you." I smirk and follow her, watching her ass jiggle slightly with each step. I groan as my dick stirs to life.

Dove turns on the shower and steps under the spray as soon as the water is hot enough. I lose my boxers and join her in the large double showerhead stall. Taking one of the washcloths, I soap it up and start washing Dove's body gently while she washes her hair.

"This feels nice," Dove murmurs. "I didn't want to admit it before, but I like you taking care of me."

"And I love taking care of you. I won't ever stop either."

After I've washed every inch of her beautiful body, she takes the washcloth from my hand and does the same for me. Washing me from head to toe, being extra gentle around my fresh shot wounds. My cock is rock hard by the time we rinse off, but I know Castro is waiting, and I'd like him in a good mood since I'm going to tell him we're leaving today.

We step out of the shower, and I wrap Dove up in an oversized towel before drying off myself. We get dressed quickly and head downstairs even though Dove's long dark hair is still wet.

When we get to the bottom of the stairs, Karl meets us and takes us to the dining room. Castro is already sitting at the table. In front of him, a colorful spread of breakfast food. There are only three plates on the table, but food to feed about thirty mouths.

"Good morning," Castro greets. "Please, sit, make yourself at home."

"Why did you want us at breakfast?" I ask bluntly as I take the seat next to Matteo.

"To see my daughter for one..." Matteo curls his top lip, but he's going to have to do better than that if he wants to scare me. I've taken tougher shits than him. I've ripped out men's organs and strangled them with them.

"We're happy to have breakfast with you, but after that, I'm taking Dove away from here. She doesn't belong here, and she wants to go home."

Matteo seems confused, which is weird because I'm pretty sure I spelled it out clear as day to him. "You seem to still be under the impression that you make the rules. It's you who owes me, and as for Dove, she's a big girl and can make her own decisions—"

"I want to go home," Dove interrupts Matteo.

Castro throws back his head and laughs. "You are home now, Daughter. At last, you're home. You're the heir to the Castro empire. My only child."

Dove visibly shudders at the word *heir*. She is clearly uncomfortable, and I know she wants to speak up, but she refrains.

He must think he's so smart, that he's pulled the cloth right over my eyes by helping me save Dove, little does he know, I see right through his bullshit exterior. He doesn't want a relationship with her. He wants to use her, and I'm going to figure out in what way.

"I know you're up to something, and I don't like it. I smell bullshit."

Matteo chuckles. "I only smell bacon, my friend... speaking of, could you hand me some."

I take my fork and spear a few pieces of bacon with it, imagining I was stabbing Matteo's eyeball instead. He takes the bacon from my fork with his meaty fingers and shoves it into his mouth.

"So, you're really going to stick to the story that all you want is to have a relationship with your daughter?"

"Of course, I want more than that. I want her to be part of the family, part of the business. I want her to continue my bloodline. Marry and give me grandchildren to lead the next generation..."

The clang of a fork hitting the plate fills the room as Dove's silverware slips from her shaking hand.

"I know it's a lot to take in and get used to, but you'll be fine, child. You're my daughter, after all."

"I don't want to be part of any of this, and I definitely wouldn't want my children—if I would choose to have any—to be part of this either."

Matteo sighs heavily, his eyes gleam with danger. He is clearly annoyed with Dove's outburst. "I don't care what you want. You are my flesh and blood, and you will do what's best for the family."

"Don't fucking talk to her like that," I growl, slamming my fist onto the table. Silverware and expensive china rattle from the impact.

Matteo turns his attention to me, pinning me with a murderous gaze. "Let's be very clear, Zane, the only reason you are still here—inside of *my* house—is to make the transition for Dove easier. If you don't behave yourself, I will have you removed, and Dove will have to figure things out the hard way. Am I clear?"

My jaw hurts from grinding my teeth, and my muscles ache from exercising restraint when I give him a slight nod. He grins, and I have to look down at my plate before the last shred of my control is gone. *Motherfucker*. He'll pay for this. He. Will. Pay.

I take a deep breath and look up at Dove. I expect her to be terrified, maybe cry. Instead, she surprises the hell out of me by swallowing her emotions and putting her game face on instead.

"Maybe we got off on the wrong foot," she announces. "Like you said, I'm not used to all of this, and it will take me a while to adjust to the idea of me having a family. I've been on my own for most of my life, and Zane has been in my life the longest. If you want me to marry him and have children, then so be it."

"Oh, child." Matteo chuckles deeply. "You won't marry him, of course. You have to marry one of my men. Someone I trust."

I'm going to kill him. I don't know when and where, but he just signed his death certificate. He'll die by my hands, and it will be a painful death.

I look at Dove across the table and see the flicker of fear in her eyes. It kills me, rips a hole in my chest. I want to kill Matteo now, jam the knife next to my plate in his throat and watch him bleed out on the white tablecloth.

But I know his men would kill me after. I'd never get Dove out of here alive, and that thought is the only thing stopping me from acting on instinct.

Surprising me, yet again, Dove remains calm. "I love Zane. I don't think I can marry someone else. There must be another way."

"Love will get you killed in this business, child. I need you to marry someone that can be head of the family business, someone strong, a leader, not a hitman from one of my rivals. That's never going to happen." He pauses, and for a moment, it is painfully silent in the room, then Matteo continues, "Look, the best I can do for you is let Zane keep working for me. He can even be your guard. Which will work out great, since I know he would die to protect you. Hell, I don't even care if you two keep fucking as long as you play the dutiful wife for everyone else to see."

I open my mouth, about to say something when I see Dove shake her head across the table. Forcing the words back down, I sit silently instead.

"Can you just give me some time? I don't know anything about this family yet. I don't even know you. Can we take this slow?"

"Of course. It's not like I'm planning on dying any time soon."

You should be, old man. Because I'm planning your death right now.

10

Dove

After breakfast, we retreat to our bedroom. Zane is quiet the entire walk back upstairs, and I feel myself imploding from the inside out. So many things just happened.

My father... if I can even call him that, told me that he wants me to marry and have children with a man of his choosing. He's made it incredibly clear that if things don't go the way he wants, if Zane tries to interfere, he'll retaliate. My mind is spinning.

He thinks he can control me, make choices for me, but he doesn't even know who I am. I'm going to have to play by his rules until I come up with a plan, but the second I figure something out, I'm gone.

When we reach the bedroom and walk inside, Zane closes the bedroom door behind us, flicking the lock into place. A gasp escapes my lips when I'm pinned to the nearest wall. Lifting my head, my gaze collides with his. Fiery rage flickers deep in those depths. I can see his pain, feel his rage as he lifts his hand, and gently strokes my cheek.

"All I could think about while we were down there was how he planned to marry you off to another man, and how I will do every-thing in my power to stop him from doing so." His teeth are clenched so tightly the words come out clipped. "I can't let him take you from me. I didn't do everything I've done, fight tooth and nail, barter, and beg to get you back, only to have you given to another man."

The pain and anguish in his voice feel like a dull butter knife cutting through my flesh. Placing my hands against his chest, I fist the fabric and tug him closer. "I'm not going anywhere, and I'm not marrying anyone. All he's trying to do is get you to react. You should know, I won't just do what I'm told."

A hint of a smile creeps onto his lips. "Oh, I know you don't do what you're told, but that's with me. How do I know you won't bend to his will if he threatens me, if he tries to hurt me or someone else you care about? I won't put you through that. You aren't any safer here than you were with Christian or Xander. We're leaving, and we're doing it tonight."

Swallowing around the thick knot that's formed in my throat, I ask, "Tonight?"

"Yes, tonight. We aren't staying here another night." I'm not sure we should try an escape so soon.

Part of me thinks Matteo will expect it, but part of me feels that if I tell Zane we can't leave yet, he'll think I want to stay when really I want to put as much distance between us and this house of terror as I can.

Ghosting his lips against my forehead, he pulls back and walks over to the window. He pulls the curtain back and peers outside. Slivers of sunlight enter the room but disappear when he lets the curtain fall closed. Turning back toward me, determination oozes from his pores. His gaze is hard, and I know there isn't any point in trying to sway him.

"We'll spend the day biding our time. Come nightfall, we'll leave."

"Okay." I nod. I don't tell him how nervous I am, or that I feel like something bad is going to happen. It's probably nothing. Or at least, I hope it isn't.

∼

BY THE TIME NIGHT FALLS, I'm a nervous wreck, but Zane has shot down any of my reasonings. I tried my best to talk him out of this, but nothing has worked.

"It's time," Zane says, tugging me to the door. "Remember, stay behind me."

I nod and follow behind him as he steps out of the room. We find the hallway quiet and empty, but we both know that Matteo's guards are around here somewhere. I haven't noticed any cameras inside this place, but that doesn't mean there are none. Maybe he's just good at hiding them. We have to be fast and precise because we'll likely only get one shot at this.

On light feet, we walk down the hall, about halfway down the stairs, we catch sight of one of the guards. Luckily, he is facing away from us, so we have the element of surprise going for us. Silently and fast as lightning Zane rushes toward him.

The guard doesn't see us coming, and Zane has an arm wrapped around his throat, squeezing the life out of him before he can make a single sound.

Shocked, I watch as Zane with nothing but a void expression in his eyes, chokes the man to death. I watch as he struggles until his body slowly sags to the floor. Strangely, I know I should feel some type of remorse, feel sadness, or at least some shame watching this happen right before my eyes. The truth is, I feel neither. At this moment, I'm numb, the void of feelings is confusing, but also liberating.

When the man lies dead on the floor, Zane searches him and takes his gun, giving me the sign to keep going. My feet move on their own, following Zane to wherever he is leading us.

Tiptoeing down the stairs, we make it through the kitchen and to the backdoor. There is no noise, no talking, nothing that makes me believe someone has seen us, but not seeing any other guards raises a huge red flag. When Zane turns the door handle, and we find the door unlocked, I really start to get worried. Can we really have that much luck? *I doubt it.*

It's like we're waiting for the other shoe to drop, the only question is, when? Hesitantly, I follow him outside and into the darkness. There is no light, only the stars above to guide the way. Through the darkness, Zane finds my hand, intertwining our fingers, and together we run across the lawn to the nearest line of trees.

Fear and adrenaline pump through my veins, and we're so close to freedom I can almost taste it. We keep moving, getting further and further away from the house, but not far enough away before all hell breaks loose. Loud yelling carries across the yard and through the trees from the house, it has us both looking over our shoulders.

The once dark house is now lit up like a Christmas tree. Every room in the house has its lights on. The doors and windows are being opened, and men in troves start storming out the back door that we escaped from.

Shit. I knew it was too good to be true.

With a panicked expression, Zane turns to me. "Run!" he whisper-shouts, already pulling me away. Racing through the wooded area, low hanging limbs whip across my face, scratching my skin. The adrenaline coursing through my veins, keeps me from feeling the pain yet, but I already know it's going to come later.

We run until we get to a large wrought iron fence, built in a way that makes it impossible to climb, leaving us with only one way to go. To run along the edge of it and find an end. We don't get far before we spot a guard tower ahead. Spotlights move across the lawn, searching for us like magnifying glasses.

"Let's backtrack," Zane says, the uncertainty in his voice is hard to miss.

We spin around, ready to head back the way we came when we see them. A couple yards away, some men are walking, they're headed right toward us, the beams of light from their flashlights flicker as they close in on us.

Fear bubbles up inside of me. Now we have nowhere to go. We're surrounded, trapped like mice. Apparently, Zane isn't as worried, or maybe he is just better at hiding it because his face doesn't show an ounce of fear. Instead, he acts like we're playing a fun game, rather than one that could get us both killed.

"Hide behind that tree," he orders, pointing to a group of trees a short distance away before heading straight for the search party.

"Zane," I hiss through my teeth, but he must not hear me calling his name because, like a rocket, he's off, charging toward the group of men like a Viking.

Turning on the balls of my feet, I run in the direction he pointed. Flattening myself against the tree, I push my back into the bark and listen to the sound of men fighting. Skin hits skin, and grunts and groans fill the brisk air, making my heart race faster with each passing second.

We aren't going to escape, there's no way.

Lights flicker over where I'm hiding, and I spot more coming our way. Do I run or stay hidden? I decide to run. Twisting around, I step away from the tree just to come to a sudden halt once more. Ice fills my veins when I see three of Matteo's men pinning Zane to the ground.

"I will fucking kill you," he growls as he struggles against them. His voice is so vicious and dark, it even terrifies me.

Through the tree branches, I can see Matteo walking across the yard. It's hard to make out his features, but even from a distance, I can make out his angry scowl.

"Find the girl! No one leaves this property until I say so." Matteo's venomous voice carries into my ears, and terror trickles down my spine. We never should've run. Looking back at Zane, something shiny catches my eye. A gun or knife. I don't know. All I know is I can't lose him. I can't risk him dying, not after I've just found him again.

My heart lurches into my throat, and even though I shouldn't, I run toward him, instead of remaining hidden.

"No! Please, don't shoot him. I'm right here," I yell over the chaos that's surrounding us.

"No! Run, Dove," Zane yells, but I refuse to escape this place without him. Matteo will kill him in an instant.

"Please, please..." I beg as one of Matteo's men points the gun at Zane while two others hold him to the ground.

I reach them at the same time my father does, the look of disappointment in his eyes would leave me feeling guilty as hell if I actually gave a shit about what he wanted or thought. Another man comes out of nowhere and circles my wrist with his hand like a shackle.

"Don't fucking touch her," Zane grits out. Even with a gun pointed at his head, his biggest concern is me. "I swear to god if you don't remove your fingers, I will cut off every fucking one of them and feed them to you."

"I think that's the least of your worries right now," Matteo sneers, frustration overtaking his features. It's hard to believe a man so cunning, so violent is my father.

"I'm sorry," I tell him, knowing and feeling that something bad is going to happen, deep down in my gut. We aren't going to get away with trying to escape. There will be consequences, grave ones. I just don't know how badly they will be yet.

"No, you're not. But you will be shortly." Matteo doesn't even look at me as he speaks. "Take them downstairs," he orders his men before turning around and walking back inside.

The men holding down Zane grab him and pull him up off the ground. While another comes and grabs me by the other arm, now I'm held on each side. They drag us back toward the house, and I've never felt more like a prisoner in my life. Fingers dig into my biceps, and I want to struggle—to kick and scream, but it would do me no good.

I'm a bird caught in a cage, my wings clipped, my spirit gone.

Directing us around the side of the house, the men open a side door. They enter with Zane first and then me. Sweat beads against my forehead, and my body feels like a knot tied into a pretzel. They release both of us, and instantly, Zane is off the floor and rushing toward me. His hands move over my face, down my shoulders and arms like he's searching for injuries.

"I'm okay," I say when I see the panicky look in his chocolate brown eyes. His only fear is losing me, or someone hurting me, and my only fear is the same happening to him.

"Who will be taking the punishment for disobeying me?" My father's deep unapologetic voice pierces my ears, and in a second, Zane turns from the comforting boyfriend into a vicious guard dog. Turning to face my father, he shields my body with his.

"Hurt her, and I will kill you in the most painful of ways you can imagine." The rage and anger. It erupts out of Zane like a volcano exploding. The burning hot lava licking at my heels.

"You're talking a lot of shit for someone that's alive because I'm allowing him to be."

"You aren't allowing shit," Zane spits.

The tension grows thicker with each word that's spoken, and I have to try and diffuse the situation before Zane gets hurt or worse killed.

"Please," I beg, stepping from behind my guard dog, and instead, to the spot beside him. Matteo turns his hardened gaze to me.

"The first thing you'll learn about us Castro's is that we don't beg, not for mercy, and definitely not for forgiveness. Now, tell me, will it be you, my sweet daughter, or will it be your junkyard dog of a boyfriend that takes the punishment."

"Me!" Zane and I both say in unison. I can feel his eyes shooting daggers into me.

"How cute, you're trying to protect each other. Funny, neither of you know what you're protecting the other from."

"Whatever punishment it is, I'll take it." The words rush out of Zane's mouth, and Matteo lets out a chuckle of amused laughter.

"Here is the deal…we aren't going to play games all night as my patience for your bullshit is running thin." One of the guards hands him a long stick, that looks to be made of bamboo. *What is he going to do?* Quivering with fear, I take a step back. "I'm going to cane one of you. If Dove decides to take the punishment, she will receive one strike. If you decide to take it, you will receive ten. What's it going to be?"

"I'll do it," I say, my voice trembling. "Zane is still healing from the gunshot wounds. Let me do it. Please!"

"You will fucking not!" Zane's voice booms through the space as he shoves me backward. The anger in his voice triumphs any sound I've ever heard. Before I can object or make a move, he's tugging his shirt off and walking over to Matteo.

"Stand with your hands against the wall," he orders Zane, whose movements are now robotic, almost as if he's shut down. It feels like I'm watching this from outside my body. Lifting the cane, he continues, "This is your only warning. If you try and fight me, Dove will incur the same punishment. Do you understand?"

Zane merely nods, his head tipped forward, his chin tucked into his chest. All I see at that moment is William. Protecting me. Saving me.

"No! Please, don't do this. Please, we won't do it again, I swear." The words tumble out of my mouth as I rush toward my father, but before I reach him, an arm circles my waist and pulls me backward.

Without even looking at me, the monster of a man called my father says, "This is your first lesson, sweetheart. Sometimes, mistakes are made, and sometimes, you make a bad choice, and others pay the consequence. Learn from your mistakes."

Without warning, he brings the cane down on Zane's back. The sound is heartbreaking, and I fight with all my might against the man holding me back, but it doesn't do me any good. He just tightens his hold on me. Kicking and screaming, I watch through teary eyes as Zane takes each lash of the cane on his back as if it's nothing. As if he doesn't feel the pain at all.

His hands ball into tight fists but remain against the wall. How can he do this to him? How can he beat someone without blinking? At the fourth strike, his skin starts breaking and blood trickles down his back. My throat is raw, and my lungs burn by the time the beating is over.

As soon as the last lash is delivered, the guard releases me. Anger flows freely through my veins, overtaking the sadness that was just there. I want to hurt all of these men, destroy them, make them pay for what they've just done.

"I hate you! I hate you so much. You will never be my father. Never," I scream at Matteo as I rush to Zane, who sags to the floor in defeat. His back a bruised and bloody mess.

"Hate me all you want, Daughter, but you will learn to follow my rules and learn to obey me, or more punishments like tonight will occur."

I don't bother responding to him, and he doesn't wait for me either. Handing off the cane to one of his guards, he shoves his hands into the pockets of his sleep pants and walks up the stairs. At the top, he turns around, and his eyes are like knives driving into my still-beating heart.

"Try and escape again, and you won't like what happens, Dove."

I steal my spine and curl my lip. "You don't own me."

"Ha, but I do. I created you, which means I'm your god," he says and disappears into the house. His men slowly filter out, and I remain sitting on the cold hard ground beside Zane, listening as his breaths turn from ragged to nothing but a wheeze.

"I'm sorry, Zane. I let you down. All over again, you saved me, and I let you down." I tell him as I softly cry, the tears cling to my eyelashes, making it hard for me to see.

Out of nowhere, a hand cups me gently by the cheek, and Zane's dark gaze bleeds into mine. "You didn't let me down, birdy. I'd endure any pain and go through any beating just to make sure you don't have to. It would kill me to see you broken and hurt. I know you wanted to protect me tonight, but you don't have to. It's my job to protect you, not the other way around." And that's when it hits me. The only way we're going to make it out of this safe and sound is if I save us. Zane might hate what's to come, but I'll do anything I have to in order to protect him, the same way he's protected me.

"Maybe I don't want to be saved anymore. Maybe I need to be the one to do the saving," I reply hoarsely.

There is something so pure, so heartwarming about the way he looks at me then. Like I'm his entire world, and he is the moon forever circling around me.

"That will never happen with me by your side. I was put on this earth to protect you, and I will do so until the moment I take my last breath."

It's then that I realize Zane's love for me would always over-shadow his choices. At any and all cost, he would choose to protect me. But I was done being the princess who needed protection. After watching him take a beating for me tonight, I will no longer play such a role. The future is mine, and I am going to be my own knight in shining armor.

11

Zane

Every muscle in my body aches, my back feels like it's been run through a shredder, but I refuse to show the amount of pain I'm in. I refuse to let Matteo or Dove see me this way. It's a weakness I cannot afford right now.

I did the right thing, taking the fallout for our failed attempt at escaping. I was stupid, careless in my planning, and I could've gotten Dove hurt in a way that I'd never be able to forgive myself for doing. Every strike of the cane, every burst of pain, was well deserved. Plus, if I had seen Dove take even one strike, it would have hurt me so much more. Maybe not physically, but mentally it would have been excruciating.

Stepping out of the shower, I dry off carefully. It's been three days, and the skin on my back is starting to scab over. Not only does it still hurt, it fucking itches now too.

The bathroom door opens slightly, and Dove's appears, looking inside like she is wondering what I'm doing in here, unsure if she is allowed to look. Instantly, my mood lightens.

"Let me help you," she whispers, stepping into the room. She takes the towel from my hand and starts carefully dabbing at my back.

I'm so enthralled by the simple gesture—by her wanting to take care of me—that the pain just falls away as if it wasn't there in the first place.

"Come, let me put some ointment on your back," Dove says, tugging me to the bedroom.

I get on the bed and lie down on my stomach. Dove gets a first aid kit from the bathroom and sits down next to me on the bed. Turning toward her, I watch with fascination as she gets out a small tube from the bag. She puts some on a piece of gauze and starts to gently cover my injured skin with a thin layer. Dove isn't even comparable to others. She's unique, in scent, style, and just overall being the woman that I love.

"That feels nice," I murmur.

"Is it not hurting still?"

"No, not right now. Your hands on me will always feel good, no matter why or how they are touching me."

"So, you do like me taking care of you?" She raises an eyebrow, challenging me.

"I do... but that doesn't mean I'll ever stop taking care of you first. You'll always be first. You deserve that," I tell her honestly.

"And what do you deserve?"

"Nothing. Not even you, but that doesn't mean I'll give you up. I will still have you. Whether I deserve you or not."

She leans down and places a soft kiss on my shoulder. "Good, because I don't want you to give me up. In return, I'll never give up on you."

I smile back at her, ready to pull her into my arms and peel every piece of clothing off her body when an annoyingly loud knocking interrupts our little bubble of momentary happiness.

"What?" I'm still completely naked, but I really don't give a shit when the door opens. I sit up and find Alberto stepping into the room.

"Fucking Christ, put some pants on," he growls, his eyes bulging out of his face before he shields his eyes with his hand.

"What do you want?" I ask, not making a move to cover up. Luckily for him, Dove is completely dressed, or I'd be gouging his eyes out right now.

"Matteo has a job for you. Get ready. And by ready, I mean fucking dressed."

"Get the fuck out!" I yell, just as he grabs the door handle and slams it shut. Turning back to face Dove, I don't miss the frown on her delicate face. She should never be sad. I want to see her smiling, always smiling.

"Don't fret, baby. I'll be back in bed with you tonight."

"I know. I just don't want anything to happen to you and..." She trails off, her cheeks tinting a soft pink.

"You what?"

"I wish I hadn't fought you so hard when we were back in the bunker at the farmhouse." Her admission warms me from the inside out. It's because of her that I haven't completely gone off the rails, why I'm taking orders from this wannabe mob boss, and why the prick is still alive. Everything I do is for her, and always will be.

"We have forever, Dove, we just have to get through this place first."

~

I'm covered from head to toe in blood. I'm not sure which is mine and which is my enemy's. All I know is that every one of those bastards is dead, the life drained right out of their bodies. Sighing, I squeeze the steering wheel a little harder. Tonight was a bloodbath, and all I want to do is get back to the house, clean myself up, and see Dove.

I can still feel her soft kisses on my skin from hours earlier. I try not to think about the fact that Matteo set me up. The fucker sent me into a fight that most men never would've gotten out of alive. Thank fuck, I'm not most men. I had years of experience, killing and shutting myself down to use nothing more than my basic instincts. There wasn't anything I couldn't handle, tonight though, that was a trap.

A dirty fucking trap, and I was going to confront Matteo the second I saw him. Pulling the SUV into the driveway, I drive to the garage, put the thing in park, and kill the engine. Giving myself a moment to cool down a little before I get out, I focus on my breathing.

Sucking air deeply into my lungs, I let it settle before blowing it out. I do this a couple more times and then finally get out. There are a few of Matteo's men posted outside. Since our attempt at escaping, he's upped security a crazy amount. Not that any of his men could take me on by themselves and survive.

"Holy shit!" one of the men says under his breath as I pass him, entering through the side door of the house. I don't respond and continue walking. Exiting the garage, I enter the house and hear voices. My bloodied boots squeak against the pure white marble floor with each step I take.

"You need to eat more. You're far too skinny, Dove," Matteo's villainess voice pierces my ears, and I walk a little faster, following the sound. Rounding the corner, I enter the dining room but come to a screeching halt when I see Dove and Matteo.

Dove's gaze immediately finds mine, and her pretty pink lips part in both terror and alarm. She seems to be shocked, and her big blues, only widen further as they take in my bloodied clothes. Words of rage form against my tongue. I'm spiraling out of control like a plane that's been shot out of the sky.

This, what I'm seeing right before my eyes, is merely the icing on top of a shittastic cupcake. I want to lash out at Dove, to be angry with her for sitting and having dinner with the enemy, but the real reason for my rage sits at the head of the table, mere feet away from me.

"Care to join us?" Matteo almost snickers, but I don't miss the surprise in his eyes. He wasn't expecting me to make it back here tonight. Fucking piece of shit, coward, can't even fight me man to man, but instead, tries to get rid of me by sending me on a death mission.

"Cut the fucking shit, Matteo, and don't act like you aren't shocked that I made it out of that fucking warehouse alive. You know as well as I do, that what you sent me to do was a suicide mission."

"And yet you stand before me."

Fucking asshole.

"Next time you want to kill me, maybe do it the less cowardly way and face me, man to fucking man." I slam a fist down onto the heavy wooden table. Dove jumps at the violent move, but she should know by now, I would never lay a finger on her pretty little body, at least not one that she didn't beg me for.

"I didn't try to kill you, Zane, and I'm actually glad that you're here. I have news that I want to share with you and Dove."

I look to Dove, who looks back at me with the same confused expression. Okay, so neither of us know what this fuckhead's next move is going to be. *Great.*

"What is your announcement?" Dove asks, her voice strong. She is not a little bird trapped in a cage anymore. Not that I mind. I'll take her any way I can get here. It's just right now, she seems fierce like a warrior, and all she's done is ask a question.

"I've decided that it's time to announce your appearance to everyone. We're going to have a special event to celebrate your return home."

My anger only intensifies at his words. He had tried to kill me and was sitting here with my girl at dinner, planning a fucking party.

"Splendid." The single word drips with sarcasm from my lips. "I'm going to go clean the blood, of the five men you sent to jump me, off my body and head to bed," I sneer and turn on my heels. My eyes catch on Dove, and her mouth pops open. She wants to say something, but I don't want to hear it. Seeing her tonight, watching her play the part of his precious little daughter, makes me want to hurt her. To set her straight and remind her just who owns her body, mind, and soul. It feels like a knife is being plunged into my chest when I drop my gaze and walk away, but I can't stand there for another second.

"Trouble in paradise already?" Matteo's voice reaches my ears just as my foot graces the first step of the staircase. I could turn around and say something to him, react to his asshole ways, but I'm too fucking exhausted to keep up the charade, so I continue up the stairs.

When I reach the bedroom, I strip out of my bloody clothes, leaving a trail behind me as I enter the bathroom. Turning the hot water on, I wait a second before stepping beneath the spray. The water feels like razor blades against my aching back, but I withstand the pain, my head hung low as I watch the clear water turn pink and rush down the drain.

The door opens, and my ears perk up at the soft footfalls. I don't turn around to look at Dove, but I can feel her in the room, watching me through the fogged-up shower stall. No matter what, I always feel her, it's truly the only thing that I allow myself the pleasure of enjoying. Her body, her touch. Turning into the spray of the water, I wet my hair, running my fingers through the strands before taking a step back.

I'm not sure what Dove is doing, so I'm surprised when the shower door opens, and she steps in behind me.

Her small hand lands on my shoulder, her fingers gently drag down my arm, and a shiver of pleasure runs down my spine. I turn to face her, ready to ask her what the hell that shitshow downstairs was, but the words lodge in my throat when she sinks to her knees before me.

"What are you doing?" I croak, the mere image before me making my cock twitch.

"Making you feel better... taking care of you," she says, a hint of a smile on her lips. She is either nervous or excited because her chest is rising and falling rapidly while she peers up at me, through her thick lashes. I'm going to go with the second, with the way her perky nipples are hardening.

She reaches for my already stiff cock, wrapping her small soft hand around it. Pleasure shoots through my body, like a bolt of lightning, pushing the pain and the anger into the deepest corner of my mind. Placing my hand against the tiled wall, I groan. Fuck, she knows just how to make me forget.

Leaning in, she takes the head of my cock between her plump lips and runs her tongue along the bottom. My dick is so hard; veins have started pulsing over the smooth skin. I'm barely controlling myself at this point, but I don't want her to stop. I need her mouth, her touch. Looking down, I watch as she starts bobbing her head, taking me deeper and deeper into her hot wet mouth, while keeping her eyes on me.

Control. I need it. Weaving my fingers through her hair, I fist the strands and pull her head back off my cock.

"I'm going to fuck your mouth, hard and fast, and you're going to let me because you're mine to use as I please, correct?"

Licking her lips, Dove nods her head before whispering, "Yes."

Guiding her mouth back to my cock, I hold her head in place and start to fuck her mouth with slow leisurely strokes. One of her hands slips between her legs, and all I can do is grin. Such a greedy fucking girl.

"Stroke your pretty pussy while you suck on my cock, and remember who it is that owns you," I grit, my voice filled with venom. Pistoning my hips, I up my pace, the tip of my cock hits the back of her throat, and she gags around my length. Her eyes water and fear trickles into her eyes as I hold her face there, my cock deep in her throat.

"Breathe through your nose, baby, and swallow with each stroke," I demand, tightening my grip on her hair as I pull her off my cock. Saliva drips out the side of her mouth and down her chin. Damn, she looks so beautiful like this. At the mercy of my cock.

Continuing to fuck her mouth, I watch and marvel as she gags around my length a few more times before following my directions. Pleasure builds at the bottom of my spine and builds upward until there is nothing but a burning in my balls to release my load into her mouth.

"I'm coming," I groan.

"Mmmm," she whimpers around my length.

"You're going to swallow every drop, do you understand?" I warn. She merely whimpers, and seconds before I explode, I hold her face to my groin. Ropes of sticky come slip down her throat as she swallows around my cock, and I pull out of her mouth, dragging my tip over her lips before releasing her. Her eyes shimmer with tears, and her lips are swollen, and fuck, I want to be inside her pussy right now, but more than that, I want her to know who it is that owns her. Tugging her up off the floor, I drop to my knees before her and back her up against the tiled wall.

"Zane, what are you doing?" She gasps as she hits the wall, and I smile up at her before lifting her by the ass and burying my face between her legs. It doesn't take long for her to get the picture, and with my tongue flicking against her clit, her legs start to shake, her fingers sink into my hair, and she shatters into a million little pieces.

When I'm finished licking every drop of her release away from her pussy and teasing her, I set her back on her feet and stand to my full height. Then I grip her by the chin and force her to look me in the eyes.

"No matter what happens, you're mine, forever. I don't care who your father tries to marry you off to. I don't care what happens in this mansion. At the end of the day, there is only you and me. I own your fucking soul just as you own mine. Don't tempt me to prove it to you again, because next time, I won't take mercy."

Dove's big blues widen, and I see something that looks like excitement in them.

"I love you," she says softly, her eyes dropping down to my chest. I release her chin and run my fingers down her chest, stopping at the scar along her belly. Back and forth, I move my finger. That scar is what binds us together. It's what made me believe she was it for me. No one ever cared about me, not until she came along.

"I love you too," I say, letting out a sigh before kissing the tip of her nose.

The problem is, I love her too much, and that just might be what gets me killed.

12

Dove

I try not to be bothered by the loneliness I feel, trapped in this stupidly large mansion while Zane is off doing god knows what for my father. It'll be a long time before I forget the bloodied mess he showed up as the other night.

This place is a thousand times worse than the bunker. At least there, Zane and I were alone, and there wasn't a knife hanging over our heads, threatening to fall and severe our necks at any given second.

Tossing the paperback down on the mattress, I climb out of bed and exit the room. Since our attempted escape, Matteo has posted more guards near our bedroom and throughout the house. Almost as if he thinks we're stupid enough to try again. I haven't told Zane yet, and I don't know if I'm going to, but I plan to be the one to get us out of this mess.

And the easiest person to start with is the one who holds all the power: my father. Meandering down the hall, I pass a couple of guards who are posted there. They give me apprehensive looks, but don't say anything as I continue on my merry way.

Walking down the grand staircase, I run my hands along the banister. The polished wood is so shiny, I can almost see myself in it, and I wonder briefly how long the maids spend cleaning this place? Reaching the last step, I continue my exploration of the house and head into the dining area. Yet another clean room. Huffing, I walk in the direction of Matteo's office.

A sour film coats my mouth, and it feels like I'm betraying Zane by seeking Matteo out. There isn't any way around it. If I want to convince him that I'm on his side, that I'll follow his orders, I'm going to have to act like I give a shit about him and what he says.

Tiptoeing down the hall, I grow closer to his office. Matteo's voice filters out into the hall through the partly open door. He must be on the phone with someone.

"Make sure the product is as he said and only call me if you have a problem!" The finality in his words makes me shiver. A man like Matteo has no cares, no compassion or heart. All he sees his people as—including me—are pieces on a chessboard, little does he know, he's going to become my pawn. Curling my hand into a fist, I gently lift it and bring it to the door, knocking twice before letting my hand fall back down to my side.

"Come in," he grumbles, and I force a stoic mask onto my face. *Be strong. Look the part.*

Exhaling, I walk into his office. His beady eyes flick from annoyance to shock while motioning me into the room. I take slow, hesitant steps, remembering how I told him I hated him and would never be his daughter. Look at me now, buttering up the enemy, like he didn't arrange to have the shit beat out of the man I love the other night.

"What can I do for you, my daughter?" I do my best not to look as out of my element as I truly feel.

"I want to learn more about you and the family business."

Chuckling, he leans back in his chair, a brief second passes, where neither of us says a thing. Then his lips part, and he asks, "You're serious?"

"You said I'm your only heir and that I should prepare to take over the family business, so here I am."

The chair squeaks as he leans forward, placing his elbows on the desk, clasping his hands together. "You expect me to believe that you want something to do with me after what you told me in the basement?"

I shrug. "When you hurt people I care about, you should expect me to lash out. I was hurt and understandably so, but I've come to the conclusion that you aren't ever going to let me go so I might as well stop fighting the inevitable. It's time I stepped up to the plate. You want me to marry soon and produce grandchildren. This business will be mine someday, and I have a right to know all the ins and outs."

The apprehension in his face tells me he doesn't believe me. A smile creeps onto his lips, and I swallow thickly, unsure if I can follow through with this.

Staring me in the eyes, he says, "I'm a lot of things, sweetheart, but I'm not an idiot. We can play pretend if you want, till you decide to get on the horse and ride, just know that I'm in control of everything and everyone in this house."

"I'm here and willing, now will you answer my questions and help me get to know you and the family better or should I try and escape again?" It's either the stupidest or smartest thing I've ever said.

Matteo's face becomes a blank canvas, and I try and hide the slight tremble of my body. Zane isn't here to save me this time, and talking like this is only going to help dig my grave. After a long second, he finally speaks.

"You know what will happen if you try and escape again, now come sit, and you can ask your questions."

Nodding, I walk to the front of his desk and plop my ass down in one of the leather chairs. Placing my hands in my lap, I slowly drag my eyes up to meet his dark ones.

"Before you tell me about the business, I was actually wondering if you could tell me anything about... my mother? What was she like? Why didn't she try and find you after she escaped her husband? What made you fall in love with her? Anything, really. I don't even know her name..."

Easing back into the chair, Matteo drums his fingers on the wooden desk. "Your mother was special. She was looking for love since her husband was more concerned with making a name for himself than being the man she needed. We met at a charity event. I saw her from across the room and knew I had to have her."

"So, you knew she was married when you met her, and you still approached her?"

Matteo nods. "I did, but it's very common in our world to be in a loveless marriage. Women are promised to men and seen as a joining of two families into one. It's more about power than anything. I didn't care that your mother was married. All I wanted was a taste."

The way he talks about my mother almost annoys me. Like she was nothing more than a piece of arm candy, or meat for him. I can tell from the tone in his voice and the use of the word taste, that she wasn't important to him. There is no love in his voice, only a sense of accomplishment. I don't know her, and I'll never get the chance to, but she's still my mother, and that fact alone means she deserves a little bit of respect.

Matteo must know I'm disgusted with him because he starts to talk again.

"Your mother's name was Raven. She told me she was going to leave her husband and wanted to be with me. Given that she was still married and divorces rarely happen, I wasn't sure we would ever be together. Then she told me she was pregnant with you. I promised her I would care for you and her if she actually decided to get away from her husband." He pauses, and I don't know if it's for dramatics or because he's reliving the day in his mind. "Then, one night, she did just that. News travels fast, her husband had men everywhere, searching high and low for her. My men came to me and told me that she had left her husband in the middle of the night, without a single trace. No one knew where she went. I waited for her, I thought for sure since she was pregnant that she would contact me, but she never did."

I can't help but feel a little sad inside. All my mother wanted was to be loved, and this viciously dark world took that chance from her.

"Where do you think she went? And why did she not call you?"

"I can't answer either of those questions. To be honest, at the time, I thought she was already dead. I was sure that her husband had caught her trying to escape and killed her. I figured he made up the whole *she ran away* and sent his men out on a search party so no one would look into her death."

"Then how and when did you realize I was alive, and she wasn't dead?"

Matteo's eyes twinkled with, no it couldn't be admiration, there was no way a man of his nature would feel such an emotion. "I may seem heartless, Dove, but I'm not. You are my daughter, and I do love you. At the end of the day, I still hung on to the sliver of hope that she had truly escaped. I hired a private investigator to keep looking for her. I told him I didn't care how long it took, months, or years, I didn't want him to stop looking for you two. Then, out of the blue, he called me. Told me that a woman fitting your mother's description was found dead in a hotel room. There was a mention of a child, a little girl. I tried to find you then, but you were already in the system, and no one would give me any information."

"Oh..." I nod as if I understand, but on the inside, I am nothing but suspicious. All the pieces of information he's given me just don't add up. I wasn't adopted until my teenage years.

I was in the system most of my life because no one ever claimed me as their family member. If he would've made himself known as my father, why wouldn't they have given me to him? The state would have been glad to have one less kid to take care of.

Matteo smiles, but it doesn't reach his eyes, letting me know it's fake. "I'm just grateful to have found you."

"But are you really grateful? I feel a little like a pawn to you."

"I only want the best, Dove. Marriage in our world is for power, so while you may be in a loveless marriage, you will be safe. I will not stop you from seeing Zane, that's the most kindness, I can give you. I've worked tirelessly to get the Castro name to where it is. When it's time for you and your new husband to take over, I want you ready, and so babying you isn't going to prepare you for what will come. Kindness gets no one anywhere."

"How will you choose the man I'm supposed to marry?"

"I need you to marry someone who will eventually take over the business, someone I trust. But I will also make sure he'll treat you well. I won't allow someone who is violent with women for no reason."

For no reason? I'm both scared and curious to hear what reasons are acceptable in his eyes. I doubt it will take much.

Wanting to keep him talking, I ask another question, "What kind of business will I be doing? I want to be involved, to know what it is you're *preparing* me for."

"You know, you don't have to be this involved in everyday dealings of the business. Your future husband can take all of this on."

"If I'm going to do this, I'm going to do this all the way. I know you don't know much about me yet, but I can tell you that I'm not the kind who sits at home and twirls her thumbs. I want to be involved, and I don't mind getting my hands dirty."

As soon as the words leave my mouth, I regret them. By getting my hands dirty, I meant it the way most people use the expression, of course, getting your hands dirty, means something else to someone like Matteo. I wish I could take back what I just said, but I can't without sounding weak.

Matteo rubs his chin. "Are you sure you're ready to hear this?"

Pursing my lips, I say, "Doesn't matter if I'm ready, does it? Eventually, I'll be running this ship, so there isn't any better time than the present. No point in easing into things. Might as well drop me off in the deep end and let me teach myself to swim."

A soft chuckle emits from Matteo's throat, and if I didn't know how fucked up he was, how willing he was to end mine and Zane's lives, I'd say this was a nice little bonding moment.

"No, sweet Dove, I will not drop you off in the deep end. I want our name to succeed long after I've died, so I'll ease you into things. Plus, the things you'll be dealing with may be a little bit of a shock to someone as sweet and naive as you. After all, you weren't born into this world." I don't miss the jab his words bring.

Wanting him to tell me something, anything at all, I push him again. "Then tell me something business-wise that's going on."

His expression becomes impassive, his dark brown eyes emotionless pits of nothing. How can he be my father? I just don't understand.

"I'm not sure you're ready for this."

"I'll be the judge of that," I say, crossing my arms over my chest. I try to make myself seem bigger than I am. Try not to let the sharks know that I'm a bloody piece of meat, barely staying above the water.

"Human trafficking. Right now, we're recruiting women and taking them to Mexico to our whore houses. They're used multiple times a day and are one of our number one profits outside of drugs."

Bile rises up my throat, and my stomach churns. Oh god, maybe I wasn't ready for this. I do my best to hide the disgust from my face.

"Where do you find them?"

Matteo smirks. "Find them? We don't find them, sweetheart. We pluck them right off the street. Kidnap them from clubs. People that owe us debts and cannot pay. We take their mothers, daughters, wives, sisters. No one is off-limits to us."

I've never heard anything so disgusting in my life. I thought Zane was mental when he told me there were worse men in this world, far worse than himself. I was naive to think that such people didn't exist, simply because I didn't see them. They were there though. Always watching, waiting in the dark for the perfect moment to ambush you.

"It's a lot to take in, so I think that is all I will share with you tonight. Maybe we can do this again?"

"Yeah, definitely," I say, pushing up and out of the chair. Can he see my fear? Feel my anger? Surely, he can, though I doubt he cares. He already sees me as weak, a naive little girl with no backbone. I can't wait to prove him wrong.

"Nice talk, now run along. I have work to do but be back down at seven for dinner," he orders in a stern voice, much like a father would talk to his daughter if she disobeyed him. My body reacts before my brain catches up, and I scurry from the room. Once in the hall, I'm tempted to turn around and go back into his office and tell him I'm not leaving because he told me to but because I'm going to be sick over what he told me but don't.

As soon as I get the chance to kill the man that calls himself my father, I will. And I won't mourn him, knowing I'll have taken another bad man off of this earth. I'll rescue all those women who he's taken and hurt, and I'll smile triumphantly while doing so.

Matteo Castro will die at my hands if it's the last thing I do.

13

Zane

Another day of killings. I don't remember a time when murdering people was ever so tiring to me. I think my biggest problem is I'm doing it for some asshole instead of myself. As soon as I enter Matteo's house, I know something is off. Voices drift from the dining room through the hallway. One is definitely Matteo, and one is Dove's, but I don't recognize the third voice at first. Not until I get closer, at least.

Clenching my fists and grinding my teeth, I walk into the house until I get to the dining room. Matteo, Dove, and Alberto are sitting around the table like they're having a fucking Sunday family dinner. Chatting and laughing casually, completely comfortable with each other. For the first time since we got here, Dove doesn't look out of place, and I don't fucking like it one bit.

What kind of game is she playing?

"Having a good ole time, I see," I say as I step further into the room. All eyes turn to me. Neither Matteo nor Alberto are even trying to hide their annoyance by my presence anymore. Dove looks at me with a mixture of guilt and apprehension. She is up to something, hiding her plans from me, and I don't like it.

"We're having a great time," Matteo says, raising his glass of wine to me. "We were just telling Dove about summers in Italy and how I'd like to take her next year."

"I would love that father," Dove chimes in. *Father? Since when is she calling him father?*

My eyes skate to Alberto, who is looking at Dove. There is a longing in his eyes that makes me want to reach out and crush him.

"Stop staring at her!" I snarl at him.

He doesn't even seem to be shocked at my outburst, which only angers me more. Does he have a fucking death wish? I'm like a damn ticking time bomb. Wonder what happens when I explode? Oh, I know...

"She isn't yours, and I can look at her if I want to. Maybe I'll even touch her?" he threatens, and I lurch toward him. I'm ready to rip his throat out when Dove's warm hand gently covers my bloodied one. Turning my icy glare to her, she meets my ice with fire.

"Enough you two. Don't act like children." Matteo dabs at his lips with a napkin before tossing it on his nearly empty plate. "You care to join us, or would you rather eat in the kitchen with the other staff?"

I'd rather slit your throat with the knife in my boot.

"I'm afraid I lost my appetite." Turning around, I head up the stairs, not stopping until I'm inside our room.

Pacing the floor, I wait for the door to open and for her to come in at any moment. When she still isn't here after twenty minutes, I fear that I made a terrible mistake. I should've stayed downstairs. Is she in danger?

I'm just about to run back downstairs when the door opens, and Dove appears in front of me.

"What the fuck was that?" I growl as soon as she closes the door behind her.

"It was just dinner, Zane."

"Don't fucking lie to me. We both know that was more than dinner. You called him *father*! What the hell are you thinking?" I throw my hands up in the air, not knowing what to do. I want to punch the wall or better, punch Alberto, but neither would end well for me.

"I'm thinking that fighting him on everything is not going to work out. He asked me to come have dinner with them, so I went. He asked me to call him father, so I did." She folds her arms in front of her body as she defends her actions.

I huff. "Oh, great, you're playing the obedient daughter now?"

"Yes! Emphasis on *playing*. Do you think I enjoyed sitting there with them, pretending to have a great time when I know you are out there in danger?" Her eyes fill with tears, but I don't know if it's because she was really worried or just because she is so angry.

"Playing or not, you are still hiding things from me. You should have told me about your plan. You should have told me your plan, so I could have told you no."

"*So you could have told me no?*" She stares at me like she can't believe what I just said.

"You heard me. You are mine, and it's my job to protect you. If I think you are doing something stupid, I'll not allow it."

"You can't control me!" Her words slam into me like a round-house kick to the chest, and something deep inside of me snaps. I take a step toward her, crowding her personal space. I raise my hand and wrap my fingers around her throat. I don't squeeze hard enough to make it difficult for her to breathe, but I tighten my grip to let her know who is in charge.

"Oh, Dove, how wrong you are," I say in a low, threatening voice. "I can control you, and I think it's time that I remind you of that. Now, take your clothes off and get on the bed."

Her eyes widen and her pupils dilate. I can feel her delicate throat work as she swallows hard before her tongue darts out to wet her lips.

Just when I think she is not going to do it, she reaches from the hem of her sweater and starts pulling it up. I release her so she can pull it off all the way. She drops it on the floor next to her and continues taking her clothes off one by one.

By the time she is naked, she steps past me and toward the bed. She climbs on the mattress, giving me a perfect view of her already glistening pussy nestled between her creamy thighs. She is turned on by this. My Dove might seek her independence in her life, but in the bedroom, she likes when I command her. She likes me controlling her.

"Stay on your hands and knees," I order as I make quick work of my own clothes.

Completely naked, I climb on the bed behind her. My heavy balls and my hard as steel cock, swaying between my legs with each move.

Positioning myself between her legs, I hold onto her hip with one hand and guide my cock to her entrance with the other. As soon as my swollen mushroom head enters her tight channel, I let loose. I sink all the way into her in one hard thrust.

I don't give her time to adjust. I fuck her hard and fast, without mercy. The sound of my groans and her pleasured cries fill the room. We are so loud; I wouldn't be surprised if Matteo hears us. Good, let him.

"That's it. Moan so loudly the whole house can hear you. Let them know whose pussy this is. Let them know how hard I fuck you and how much you like it. Let everybody hear what a slut you are for me." At my dirty words, her pussy tightens, and more moisture builds between us.

"Zane," she moans my name, and I fuck her even harder, digging my fingers into her flesh as I hold onto her, wanting and needing to bruise her.

"You're mine, Dove. I do own you. I own every part of you, and I'm going to use you however I want, remember?"

"Yes," she whimpers in between thrusts. "Yes... use me. I'm yours. Do whatever you want."

"That's right," I growl. "You take my cock, however, and whenever, I want you to."

Letting go of her hip with one hand, I move my hand to her ass and start massaging her puckered asshole with my thumb while I keep fucking her. She moans in response, letting her upper body fall onto the mattress so her ass is even further open for me.

"Your greedy little asshole wants me."

Before she can answer, I push my thumb inside, letting her hole suck me in. I start pumping in and out of her ass at the same speed my cock goes in and out of her cunt.

Her orgasm slams into her, her thighs quiver, her body tenses, and her pussy and ass squeeze me so tightly, I think I might come apart right then. It takes a lot to hold my own orgasm at bay, but I don't want this to be over. I'm not done with her by a long shot.

When the last tremor of her release leaves and her body is slack, I pull out and flip her over in one swift move. Her back has barely touched the mattress when I'm back inside of her, rutting into her like a wild animal.

I hold her legs up, pushing them toward her to give me better access. "God, your cunt is so tight this way. I bet your ass will be even tighter."

She moans in response, seemingly unable to form coherent words at the moment. Her hooded eyes glance up at me with nothing but pure lust and obedience. She is submitting to me completely, and even though it might be only in the bedroom, for now, I'll gladly take it.

"Play with your tits while I fuck you," I order, and her hands move to her breast on command. She takes her nipples between her fingers and starts playing with them, tugging and pulling harder than I would dare to.

"You like when I take you rough, don't you?" She nods her head, yes, before I've finished talking. "You like being my little fuck toy, like being used?" She nods again and whimpers, taking her bottom lip between her teeth and bites down, all while still playing with her tits.

That sight drives me over the edge, my balls tighten, and pleasure overcomes me. I come so hard my vision blurs. I keep thrusting deep inside of her as I come, shoving every drop of my come inside of her.

"Fuck!" I come until my balls are so empty it hurts. Stilling, buried inside of her, I close my eyes and take a moment to just breathe.

When I pry my eyes back open, Dove is watching me. Her hands are still on her chest, but not moving anymore. I carefully pull out of her, enjoying the sight of my come dripping out of her before I release her legs. She lets them fall to either side of me. I climb over her leg and fall onto the mattress next to her.

Even feeling sated as I am right now, the thought of her keeping things from me and being friendly with the enemy is too much to ignore.

"You're playing with fire, trying to get close to Matteo. You're gonna get burned."

"And what else am I going to do? Nothing? Fight him? Try to escape? We both know how that worked out last time." Her words sting, but she isn't wrong.

"I admit, trying to escape the way we did was a mistake. It won't happen again, but you getting close to him is a mistake as well. Let me deal with him."

"How?"

I don't really want to tell her, but I realize by not telling her, I'm doing the same thing I'm mad at her for. "I'm gathering info on Matteo to hand over to Christian. He only wanted you to get to Matteo. If I can get him a better way to get to him, then we kill two birds with one stone. Dove, you need to promise me that you won't do anything foolish while I'm out doing jobs for your father. I can't stand the thought of you hanging out with him, and Alberto like you're old friends while I'm out there. Promise me..."

Turning my head, I look over to her, she stares up at the ceiling. "I promise," she mumbles in defeat.

Now I only wish I could believe her.

14

Dove

Zane's gone again. Doing another job for my father. I feel him pulling away from me, emotionally, he's shutting down. I know he still wants me, still loves me, but the games my father is playing, it's draining him. He'll do anything to protect me, anything to try and save us from this situation when the only person who can save us is me.

I know I promised Zane I'd stop pretending with Matteo, but I just can't do it. I can't let Zane take all the responsibility. We are in this together, and I can't sit back and do nothing.

He thinks what I'm doing is risky, and it is, but sometimes there are risks you have to take. A knock sounds against the heavy wood of the door, and before I say anything, the knob twists, and the door opens, a maid's head pops into the room. She can't be but a little older than me, her heart-shaped face and almond eyes make me think she could be a model if she wasn't here working for my father. I look up at her and smile. Her expression is blank, and she doesn't return the smile, but in her eyes, I can see fear.

"Your father is requesting your presence in his office," she whispers, eyes cast to the floor. I swallow around the knot that's forming in my throat.

He's been eating up a lot of my time during the day, requesting me to eat dinner with him, which conveniently happens to fall at the same time Zane walks in the door. I know it's a set-up, a way to drive a wedge between Zane and me, and in a way, it's working.

"Thank you. I'll be right down," I say, and she closes the door quietly behind her. Sighing, I force myself out of bed and run my hands through my silky brown hair in an attempt to make myself a little more presentable. Once done, I slip from the room and walk down to Matteo's office. Guards are still posted throughout the house even though Zane and I haven't made another attempt at escaping.

I'm not sure when he will ever trust me, and he's smart not to because the instant he does, I'm running with it.

Standing just outside his office, I push the door open and listen as it creaks. Matteo looks up from something on his desk and to me as I pop my head inside.

"You asked to see me?"

He waves me inside, and I stop right in front of his desk. "Yes, I want you to go with Sophia and pick out a dress for the event. I also want you to get your hair done."

My brows furrow. "What's wrong with my hair?"

"Of all the things you can fight me on, you fight me on your hair?" He lets out a chuckle. "Just get your hair done, please. It looks dull."

I'm tempted to tell him to fuck off, but that would derail my plan completely, so instead, I bite the inside of my cheek.

"When is this Sophia woman coming?"

Matteo's gaze flicks to his watch and then back up to me. "Should be here any minute now." I nod, ready to turn around and walk out. Why subject myself to his bullshit any more than I have to. "Also, pick something out that isn't too revealing but gives a tiny peek. I want people to be talking about us for weeks to come."

"Of course," I mumble and step out of the office. I go upstairs and get a pair of tennis shoes before coming back downstairs.

Lingering in the foyer, I wait for this shopping lady to show her face. Just as Matteo claimed, she shows up a few minutes later. Priding myself on being someone who never judges a book by its cover, I try not to judge the woman who comes walking into the mansion like she owns the place, a sneer of disapproval on her face when she spots me waiting for her.

"Dove?"

"The one and only. You must be Sophia."

"That I am. Now, I'm not one for pleasantries, so let's get on with the shopping. We have money to spend and dresses to try on."

Well then. I follow her out to an SUV and climb into the back seat while she takes the passenger seat up front. One of Matteo's men drives and another comes as security. No one says anything to me the entire drive.

The rest of my day is spent trying on dress after dress while Sophia critiques every single one. *That one is way too short. Ugly. You look fat.* Are just some of the remarks I have had to withstand. By the time we're done, my ears are bleeding, and I feel like going back to the mansion and drowning myself in the bathtub, but that can't happen because first, I have to get my hair done. Sophia ships me off to the hairdresser, whose name is Bernarto.

"You're gorgeous, sweetheart," he purrs in my ear while running his fingers through my hair. For the first time all day, I smile.

"Thank you," I say.

"What shall we do..." He drums his fingers against his chin and takes a step back, eyeing my head. After the day I've had, I don't really care what he does. Making up his mind, he gets to work, and three hours later, my hair is colored, trimmed, and styled. Surprisingly, I feel a little better. Sophia scoffs when she sees me and rolls her eyes before typing out something on her phone. Then, all over again, we're getting into the SUV and heading back to the mansion.

When we arrive, I all but dart from the car, needing to put some distance between Sophia and me. She didn't say anything directly to hurt me, but she sure as hell didn't make today fun either.

Walking through the front door, I can make out the sound of voices. They're loud and manly and carry down the hall and into the foyer.

Both I know, one belonging to Zane and the other Matteo. Tiptoeing down the hall so I can hear more of the conversation, I hold my breath when Zane starts to speak.

"Fuck! I've done everything you've asked of me. All I want in return is to know that you won't marry her off to someone. Promise me you won't do it." The anguish and despair in his voice makes me take another step forward. There is a pause, and Zane starts to talk again. "If you're doing this to hurt me, then I'll break it off with her. I won't be with her anymore, but please, don't ruin her life just to get revenge against me. Dove deserves more than that."

A chair creaks, and I know it's Matteo's. "Listen here, boy. Dove is my daughter, and because of that, I get to make the rules here. She is marrying whoever I choose, when I decide. I'm not doing anything because of you. I'm doing this because it's my right as her father."

Zane growls, and I can feel the sound in my bones. "I won't let you do this. You've hurt her enough already."

Matteo chuckles, but it isn't filled with amusement, no it's the kind of humorless laugh that makes your shiver and piss yourself.

"I'm warning you now because I know Dove is fond of you, but if you interfere in any way with the plans I have for my daughter, I will have you killed and disposed of at the bottom of the harbor. Do you understand me?"

His statement sends shockwaves rippling through me. I've always known that Matteo had the power to try and take Zane out, but part of me never thought he would. Now that I've heard the words come out of his mouth, I know he'll follow through. Just like Zane won't ever give up on protecting me, making sure that my father doesn't marry me off to some man just for the sake of it.

Zane's determined, and he'll die before he ever lets Matteo do something I don't want.

"No, I don't understand, and I never will. Dove's happiness

should be your number one priority. Marrying her off to some douchebag isn't going to make her happy."

"It isn't? Are you sure about that? Are you sure it isn't you who is more worried about Dove being married? After the initial shock wore off, she hasn't voiced a single concern or complained again. Truthfully, I think the only problem is you. And we both know what must be done with problems."

Dread consumes me. I know right then and there, what has to be done and it's going to kill me. It's going to rip me to pieces, but it's the only way I can save Zane and myself. The only way I can ensure that we have even a sliver of a chance at a future together.

"Kill me, but it won't change a thing. In fact, it will only make Dove hate you more."

"I don't think so," my father says, and I'm sickened by the sureness in his voice. He doesn't know me at all, but he thinks he does, and that's my advantage in all of this. I'm playing him, and he doesn't even know it.

"By the time this is all over, you'll have made an enemy out of her." The disgust in Zane's voice can't be missed.

"We'll see," my father says.

Turning, I rush down the hall and up the stairs to our bedroom before either of them can hear or spot me. By the time I reach the room, my heart is racing out of my chest, and there are tears in my eyes. What I have to do is going to kill me, but it has to happen if my plan is going to work.

15

Zane

My blood boils in my veins, burning me from the inside out like acid. Putting on the uncomfortable suit Matteo is making me wear, I wonder how I'm going to make it through the night without killing someone. I can't fucking believe I agreed to this. Going to this event as Dove's bodyguard. Of course, it's not like I have a choice. *Fuck.*

After I slip into my shoes and clip on the tie, I leave the room and head downstairs. Dove is getting ready in one of the guest rooms on the other side of the house. Matteo had a whole crew of stylists coming to get her ready. As if she needs a spec of makeup to be the most beautiful creature at this event.

Taking a seat in the foyer, I wait for Dove and Matteo to be ready.

An involuntary growl slips out when Matteo comes down first, his hair slicked back, an Armani three-piece suit covering his body.

"Down, boy." He chuckles, only infuriating me further.

Lucky for him, I'm distracted the next second when I catch sight of Dove at the top of the stairs. I'm pretty sure my heart skips a beat. No, she doesn't need an ounce of makeup to be beautiful, but it does accentuate her beauty. She starts walking down the stairs, and as cheesy as it sounds, I feel like she is an angel descending from heaven. I stand without thinking and greet her at the bottom of the stairs.

I don't care if her father sees how awestruck I am by her. She's my one and only true weakness in life.

"You look beautiful," I say as I place a kiss on her cheek. The stylist must really know what they're doing because her makeup looks perfect, and the cream-colored dress she's wearing makes her seem virginal and pure. At this rate, I know for sure now that I'll end up killing someone tonight. Not being able to go to this stupid event as her date is going to be torture at its finest, but way better than being stuck in this mansion all night without her. With heels on, her head reaches the bottom of my chin, and I kinda like her being a little taller.

Her glossy pink lips tilt up into a smile. "Thank you, and you look rather handsome yourself." She wraps her arms around my neck and leans into me. The dress she's wearing isn't form-fitting, thank god, but it's short enough to tempt those wanting to take a peek.

"It's going to take a serious amount of effort not to strangle every motherfucker that looks at you tonight," I whisper into the shell of her ear.

"Hate to break up the lovefest, but we're on a schedule," Matteo interrupts, "also, there will be none of this at the event. You're her bodyguard. Nothing more than that."

Turning, I pin him with an icy glare. There's a glint in his dark gaze, and he's lucky, so fucking lucky, that I care more about Dove than ending his life.

Taking a step back from Dove, a mask slips over my face to cover up the raging inferno that's threatening to consume me. Every day, this asshole pry's away another piece of the delicate armor I've erected to help stop from losing my shit on him. My patience is thin, and I'm reaching the point of no return. Once I fall off the deep end, I'm not even sure Dove will be able to reach me.

Soon, there will be nothing left. No protect, no boundary, and it's then that I will end him.

"It's time to go," Matteo says, interlocking his arm with Dove's.

She frowns at me but doesn't say anything, and even though she promised me she wouldn't, I know she's still leading him on, playing with fire, so to speak. She thinks she won't get burnt, but I know better. I've done this before a time or two.

An SUV pulls up just as we cross the threshold to outside. I tug at the uncomfortable collar constricting my neck. This is going to be the longest stretch of hours of my life. Matteo being the gentlemen he so clearly isn't, opens the rear passenger side door and helps Dove in. When she's tucked away inside the vehicle, he turns to me.

"Don't do anything fucking stupid tonight, or I'll make you regret it."

"The only stupid thing I'm doing is dealing with you."

Matteo merely smirks before clapping me on the shoulder. "You have a lot to learn, and I look forward to watching you fall to your knees and beg me for forgiveness. After all, it wasn't, but a couple days ago, you appeared in my office, begging me to relieve Dove of her family duties, am I right?"

All I can do is grit my teeth and clench my hand into a tight fist because if I make the wrong move, if I do the wrong thing, it won't just be me paying the price, it'll be Dove too. Matteo releases me and walks around the SUV without another word, climbing into the back and taking the seat beside Dove.

Forced to take the passenger side seat in the front, I climb into the SUV. As soon as I look over, I feel the need to drive my fist into the window beside me. The driver is none other than Alberto, who gives me a slimy grin as soon as I'm situated in my seat.

"You look beautiful this evening," he compliments Dove as he moves the car from park and into drive.

"She really does, doesn't she?" Matteo praises from the back seat.

"Thank you, both," Dove replies timidly, and all I can hear is the blood pumping through my veins.

"Not to ruin the good mood," Matteo says, "but I want to be very clear. The building the party is held in will be surrounded by my people if either one of you steps out, they have permission to shoot you."

Don't lash out. Think of Dove. I talk myself off the ledge slowly and peer out the window, ignoring everyone, including Dove. I can't think about her, or what we're going through right now, without wanting to slaughter. For everyone's sake, including my own, I hope no one touches her tonight because I'm not sure I'll be able to stop myself from painting the room red.

∾

MISERY. That's what this party is, plain and simple misery. It takes place in a massive hall that's connected to a hotel that Matteo owns. Of course, he's invited everyone and their extended family for the homecoming of the century. It feels a little too formal for a homecoming though.

I watch from the door closets to the table Dove is sitting at. She's surrounded by Matteo's men, three on one side, while Matteo sits beside her, and another two sit beside him. She's a swan in a lake full of tar, beautiful, majestic but unable to escape her surroundings.

Our eyes collide from across the room, the heat in those blues scorch me. Her gaze lets me know the most important thing of all. That even though it seems like the world is on fire around us, she is still here, burning in the same hell right alongside me.

Dinner is served, and as her bodyguard, I watch the surroundings while she mingles and eats with her father. Jealousy is like a whip, landing against my skin every time another man takes her hand and presses a kiss to it.

MINE! She is mine. I want to scream from the heavens. Forcing

myself to look away, I scan the crowd. None of the faces look familiar, and I'm thankful for that. I wouldn't be surprised if Christian
sent some of his men here. Then again, maybe that was Matteo's
intention, after all, to bring him out of hiding.

As my eyes pass over each face, something off to the right side
of the room catches my eye. It's only a split second that I see him. I
can't be too sure, but I swear Xander Rossi disappears through the
door at the back of the room.

Why is he here? Has he come to take Dove again? Fear pumps
through me at the speed of lightning. I'm not sure if I should say
something to Matteo or not. If I can find him, maybe I can strike up
a deal with him instead.

Before I can think too long on it, Matteo is shoving out of his
chair and moving to the front of the room. He holds a flute of
champagne in his hand and smiles out into the crowd like he isn't a
shark willing to shred anyone who stands in his way.

"Good evening, and thank you so much for coming to celebrate
the return of my long-lost daughter, Dove back into my life,"
Matteo exclaims, and the room erupts in joy. "After her mother's
disappearance, I never thought I would find her, but here she is. At
last, home... where she belongs."

I roll my eyes because the only other option is barfing, and I
don't want to make a scene. My gaze darts between Dove, Matteo,
and Alberto, who not so casually slides his hand onto the back of
her chair. Dove doesn't seem aware of it, or she doesn't care, which
only enrages me further.

I'm going to kill him. Murder him. Rip out his intestines and
strangle him with them and cut up his body, and use it as shark
bait.

As I'm envisioning this, Matteo continues talking, but I'm too
far gone to care what slimy bullshit he's spewing. None of it is true
anyway.

"Tonight isn't just about the return of my daughter though. It's
also about the legacy of the Castro family. As we all know, I'm not

getting any younger, and my daughter returning to my life just happened to come at the best time."

My brow furrows as the thoughts of Alberto's death slip from my mind. My attention is once again back on Matteo.

What is this fucker doing?

Looking back at Dove, I see that she's just as confused by his speech as I am, though she could be acting the part. With her, it's hard to tell which side she's playing and when she's playing it. The room falls quiet, and my stomach twists into tight knots. I'm bracing for whatever to come, but I don't think anything could prepare me for Matteo's next words.

"I would like to announce the joining of my daughter, Dove Castro, to my finest and most fierce second in command, Alberto Salvatore, in marriage."

My vision blurs for half a second, but the bloodthirst fog over my eyes turns to mist when I feel Alberto's eyes on me. Our gazes clash, hate and venom spewing out of me, and snaking across the floor. I will make him pay. I will make all of them pay if it's the last fucking thing that I do. A shocked gasp falls from Dove's lips, but that's the only response I get letting me know that she knew nothing of this incident. Matteo blindsided both of us.

Before anyone can see Dove's shocked face, she skews her expression and pulls her lips up into a tight smile. Like the perfect fucking couple, Alberto wraps an arm around her and tugs her into his side, his lips grazing her ear.

To anyone, they look like the perfect couple, together and in love, and that's the last straw for me. I won't sit here and watch this. I can't. I already feel the bile rising up my throat, the anger in my veins fueling my rage. I have to leave before I do something stupid.

Tugging off my tie, I toss it to the ground and exit through the doors. Anger ripples through me like a seismic wave cracking through the earth. Rounding a corner, I clench my fists and try and breathe through my nose, but nothing is helping me at this point. I've left Dove back there with Alberto and Matteo, even though I didn't want to because I just can't stomach seeing it. Watching her act as if she doesn't love me, as if that shouldn't be us getting married.

Fuck! Knocking shoulders with some asshole, I continue stalking wherever the fuck it is I'm going until he opens his mouth.

"You could say excuse me," he sneers. I almost chuckle as I turn around and stare him straight in the eyes.

Cocking my head to the side, I except the challenge reflecting in his eyes. "I could, but I don't really give a fuck."

"You need to be taught a fucking lesson on manners, don't you?" This time, I do chuckle. I laugh hard enough that my abs tighten and my belly trembles. This asshole can't be but a little older than me. He's slim, with an athletic body, but he's nothing to a killer like me, and worse yet, he's just signed his own fucking death certificate.

"Don't do this, Seth." A girl tugs on his arm, her eyes pleading.

"Maybe listen to your girlfriend," I say with a sneer, nagging him on. I want him to hit me first, to make the first move because as soon as he does, I'm going to knock his lights out.

Shrugging her off like I had hoped he would, he rolls up the sleeves of his shirt and stalks toward me. Clenching his fist at his side, he rears back and aims for my face, but being the amateur that he is, he misses his mark by a mile.

My vision turns black, and all I do is react, my movements are fluid, and I'm aware that my knuckles are colliding with skin and bone, but I don't care. Screams pierce the air, pierce through my ears, but all I see in that instant is Alberto, his arm wrapped around my girl, his lips whispering into her ear.

All I see is the woman I love slipping through my fucking fingers.

16

Dove

My father couldn't have said what I think he did. My stomach churns, and bile rises up my throat at the knowledge. I do my best to keep it together, shoving all my emotions into a tight little box that I promise to let out later.

I have to be strong in front of Matteo. I can't let him know that I've been caught off-guard by his announcement. Alberto, of course, takes full advantage, leaning into my side, wrapping his arm around me as if we're a couple, and I don't want to stab him with the steak knife in front of me. His lips are so close to my ear, I can hear every inhale and exhale that passes them. "Don't look now, but your little boyfriend looks like he wants to kill me. Should I reach for your tit, or do you think that would be pushing it?"

I can't even get the word *no* to come out of my mouth before I'm shrugging his arm off my shoulder. "There is one thing Zane will always have, and that's my love." Twisting around in my seat, I glance over my shoulder and to the spot where Zane is supposed to be standing. There's no one there. The spot is empty, and I know... I just know that something bad has happened. *Where did he go?*

Panic claws at my insides, wrapping its slimy hands around my heart.

"We will have more news to share, but just know the Castro family is strengthening its ties, and soon, we will be the strongest family this side of the Mississippi." The people around us erupt with cheers, and my father descends the steps, coming back down to the table.

Pushing from my spot, I meet him around the side of the table.

"Zane is gone. I need to go and find him." I say, leaning into his face. Matteo's features become harsh, menacing.

"No, you need to worry about your obligations to this family. Zane is no one to you. In fact, I was going to wait to tell you this till after the event, but I figure there isn't any point in elongating the heartache that will ensue."

"What are you talking about?" I bite out, afraid of what he's going to say next.

He smiles, and my heart clenches in my chest. "Look, I gave this whole Zane and you having a secret relationship a chance, but obviously neither one of you can handle it. He is a liability."

"But... I don't understand. What are you saying?"

"I'm saying if you do not get rid of Zane, I will have no choice but to get rid of him. And by that, I mean, I will kill him. I honestly planned to allow him to stick around and be by your side, but his antics have made me think twice about that. He is now more of a risk than he is an asset."

Shocked, my mouth pops open before I can snap it shut. My biggest fear is now becoming my reality, and all over again, I'm faced with losing Zane.

"I..." I don't even think my brain hasn't quite comprehended what he's said yet. "I... I love him," I whisper harshly.

Matteo leans in, a single finger tracing down the side of my cheek. "I know, sweetheart, which is why I'm giving you the chance to end things with him. Make him go away so that his death doesn't rest on your shoulders because, I promise you, if you don't make him leave, I will end him myself. The choice is yours, Daughter."

The world beneath my feet shifts, and I grab onto the nearest chair to steady myself. Zane will die if I don't make him leave, but making him leave isn't going to be easy. It will mean breaking his heart. It will mean having to lie to him. Protecting him, will ultimately end everything that we have, and still, there isn't a way around it. Matteo isn't lying, there isn't a doubt in my mind that he will kill Zane. We've been heading toward this scenario since the day he went to him to rescue me.

I have to do this because the alternative is so much worse.

"I understand," I whisper to my father.

A smile splits across his face, and he nods. "I knew you would. You're a smart girl, Dove."

Before he walks away, I grab him by the arm. "Give me at least three days, please?"

Matteo looks as if he wants to say no but then opens his mouth to speak. "Three days. I'll give you three days, but that is all my little bird."

Little bird. The nickname causes a horrible reaction in my brain. The urge to vomit is strong. The mere thought of going without Zane terrifies me. It makes the game I'm playing more intense, more real, because with Zane out of the picture, the only person I'll have to save me is myself. Forcing myself to take a couple calming breaths, I resurface, realizing that I still have to play the role of Castro's obedient daughter.

For the next two hours, I think of Zane while forcing a smile onto my lips as my father parades me around like a trophy, and Alberto is slapped on the shoulder and told what a prize he snagged. By the time the sun starts setting, my father is two sheets to the wind and in a deep conversation with an allying family.

Slipping from the dining hall, I head toward the bathroom. It's been hours since I last saw Zane, and I need to find him. Deep down, I know he wouldn't leave me here. He knows I have nothing to do with this, though that wouldn't stop him from acting out on his rage and jealousy.

Around the same time he disappeared, there was a commotion

out in the garden. A man had beat the crap out of another man. Matteo's men rushed out to break up the fight, but when they arrived, the other man was already gone.

Something tells me that was Zane, and all I can do is hope that he's okay while I bide my time till I can go and find him. Walking into the bathroom, I plan to stay inside just long enough to get some of the guards off my tail, so I can start my search. Matteo's men are vigilante as hell, and getting around them has been difficult, to say the least.

Placing my hands face down on the sink, I stare at my reflection in the mirror.

Can I really do this?

I nearly lost him once before, can I be the one to push him away, to end our perfect love story? Tears sting my eyes. This isn't going to end well. Zane will see right through me, right through my lies, and deep into my soul. He'll know I'm lying, and that something else is going on. I'll have to look him right in the eyes and tell him I don't love him anymore. That I don't want him to be in my life. When that is as far from the truth as anything.

Letting him go is going to kill me, but there isn't another option.

The minutes tick by slowly, and thankfully, no one else comes into the bathroom to witness my break down. I can't possibly stay hidden in this bathroom all night. I have to find Zane and make sure he's okay, but leaving this space is subjecting myself to the mayhem beyond these four walls.

Forcing myself to leave the bathroom, I turn and walk out the door. I make it all of ten feet down the hall, my heels clacking against the exquisite floor, before a hand clamps down on my shoulder and whirls me around.

The air expels from my lungs when I'm shoved against the nearest wall, and Alberto's face comes into view.

"Hiding from me?" The whiskey on his breath tickles my nose, and I struggle against his firm grasp. His eyes are bloodshot, and I know after watching him for the last two hours, that he's had more to drink than he should have.

"No, now please, let me go," I say firmly, pushing against his chest, but pushing him is like trying to move a mountain. My movement only entices him further, and he leans in, his lips descending on mine. At the last second, I manage to turn my face, and he lands a sloppy kiss against my cheek.

"Oh, it's like that, huh? Am I not good enough for you?" His hand grabs onto my tit, squeezing painfully, and a ragged hiss passes my lips. I clench my fist and swing my arm, hitting him in the side of his head. Unfortunately, my punch doesn't have much force behind it, and since he is drunk, his pain tolerance is down. He just chuckles at my feeble attempt to hit him.

"Stop, I don't want to do anything with you until after we're married."

"Awe, why not? I know you fuck Zane." Leaning in, he drags his lips across my neck, sucking harshly.

"Stop!" I say a little louder, preparing myself to push him away, but before I can, a shadow falls over us, and Alberto is ripped away and tossed to the ground like a piece of trash.

I'm about to jump into Zane's arms, telling him how sorry I am, and that he was right about everything. Instead of lunging forward into my lover's arms, I'm frozen in place. It takes me a good second to realize it's not Zane standing in front of me but someone else entirely.

Ivan.

"I-Ivan…"

"Hello, Dove," he greets me casually as if we're two old buddies who happen to be at the same party. Peeking behind him, I notice that he is not alone. With him is a man of similar stature, who is just as scary and daunting looking as him.

"Um, hi," is the only thing I can manage to say. I'm not really sure if I should be scared or relieved to see Ivan right now. Why is he here? Surely, Matteo didn't invite him, the way he talks of the

Rossi family, I'm sure he'd rather eat his own shit than dine with them.

Behind Ivan, Alberto is trying to get off the ground. He only barely manages to stand on his own, more like swaying on his feet. He opens his mouth to say something but then stops himself when recognition sets in. Oh, he definitely knows Ivan and whoever this other man is, and from the way his body is trembling, it's clear he is scared of them.

"What the fuck are you doing here?" Alberto snarls after a moment of composing himself.

The man I don't know shrugs. "Heard there was a party, figured we'd check it out. Kinda pissed we didn't get an invite."

"Cut the crap, Roman. Why are you really here?"

"Congratulations on your engagement," Ivan says, both interrupting and changing the subject. "You seem like a *lovely* couple. Do you always have to force girls, or is there actually someone who touches your dick willingly?"

"Fuck you, Ivan," Alberto slurs before storming off. How wonderful of him to leave me standing with two giant men in an otherwise empty hallway.

"You okay?" Ivan asks a moment later, his facial features softening, but only a little.

"Yes, thank you," I reply, smoothing a hand down my dress, mainly because I need something to do with my hands.

"This is my brother, Roman." He introduces the man next to him. Ah, brothers, that makes sense now. "Why the hell are you engaged to that douche?"

"It's a long story." I shake my head, not wanting to tell him the whole story right here in the middle of the hall, where anyone could hear. "Why are you here?"

"We heard Castro was making a big public announcement. Xander wanted us to check out what he was up to. Gotta admit, I wasn't expecting this."

"Yeah. Believe it or not, I wasn't expecting *this* either."

Ivan looks shocked. "Oh, wow. Well, shit. Where is Zane?"

"Around here somewhere. I'm pretty sure he got into a fight after the big announcement."

"Well, folks, I would like to stay and chat," Roman announces, "but I think we should head out before dipshit gets back with a small army because he is too scared to fight his own battles."

"Yeah, that might be a good idea," I say, looking down the hallway to see if any of my father's men have noticed I'm missing. Now would be the perfect time to disappear, but it's not worth it, not after hearing we'll be shot without warning if we try to leave the grounds.

"Take care," Ivan says before turning to walk away. I watch them leave via the exit and then head back to the party to try and find Zane. Back in the main room, I scan the crowd. Alberto is sitting next to my father at the table. He's glaring at me like he'd like to strangle me. I'm surprised he didn't tell my father about Ivan and Roman, then again, I'm sure he doesn't want me to tell my father about what he did either.

Not wanting to sit down with them again and endure more pretending, I head to the bar. As I walk through the crowd, I notice everybody staring at me as if they're sizing me up or something. Some people actually look scared when I walk by them, making space for me to walk through.

The whole thing is surreal, and I feel nothing but out of place and misunderstood. I almost turn back around and walk back to the table out of desperation when I spot Zane at the bar. Knowing that I can't make a scene, I take the seat next to him without looking over.

"Can I get a glass of water, please," I ask the bartender whose attention I catch.

"Of course. Sparkling or still?"

"Sparkling sounds great." I barely finish my order before he produces a glass and a small bottle of water in front of me. "Thank you."

"No champagne to celebrate?" Zane whispers next to me.

"Stop it. You know that I don't want this," I say in a hushed voice, so only Zane can hear me. "Do you think I'm happy about this?" I ask and take a sip of my water.

Putting his elbow on the bar top, he lets his head fall into his hand. "I know, but that doesn't make this any easier."

"I'm going to ask Matteo to take us home. There we can talk." I get up from my seat and weave through the crowd, back to our table.

Matteo and someone I don't know, are deep in conversation when I get there. So, I tap my father lightly on the shoulder to get his attention.

He stops talking and looks up to see who dares to interrupt him. "Dove, you enjoying the party?"

"It's a lovely party, thank you for planning all of this, but I'm rather tired, and I'd like to go home. Do you mind having someone take me back to the house?"

Alberto perks up next to him. "I can take you."

"I would rather have someone less drunk take me home," I insist.

"Of course, dear. Let me get someone for you." Matteo smiles and waves over some of his men. "Take my daughter home," he orders, and the men nod.

"Thank you, Father. Enjoy the rest of your night." I force out the pleasant words when all I want to do is strangle this man with my own hands. I don't care if he is my father or if we share blood. This man is pure evil, and I'll do whatever it takes to stop him.

I follow the two men out of the main room and to the front door. By the time we make it to the car, Zane has caught up to us. We drive back to Matteo's mansion in silence, not wanting to talk in front of the men, but I know this silence will be over once we are alone.

We park right in front of the house. I get out as soon as the car comes to a standstill. Zane follows me inside the house just as my father's men do. But unlike Zane, the men stay downstairs.

When we are finally inside the containment of our room, we both sigh deeply.

"I can't do this, Dove. I can't watch you with them, with some other guy... even if you are pretending. It's like my worst nightmare playing out in front of me. I love you too much. I can't stand this. I'm scared, Dove. *Scared!* I don't even remember the last time I experienced that feeling, but I am now. I'm scared of losing you, losing us."

"I know..." My voice is raw with emotion, I'm feeling everything he just said. "I hate this too, but if I need to gain Matteo's trust. I need him to give me freedom so we can get away. If we try again now, he'll kill you, and lock me up."

Zane growls in annoyance, knowing that I'm right. Frustration and anger come off of him in waves, and I know if I don't calm him down, he is going to punch the wall or something.

"Can we just lie down so you can hold me? Please, I just need you to hold me," I whine.

Zane nods and starts taking off his clothes before helping me out of my dress. Together we crawl into bed and under the blanket. He pulls me to his chest, and I snuggle up to him as close as I can. I don't know how long I can have him like this, and for tonight, I don't want to think about this either. I let his warmth engulf me, let his unique scent calm me, and the steady beat of his heart lull me to sleep.

17

Zane

Something terrible is going to happen. I can feel it. Dove is acting stranger than usual. After the event the other night, I poured my heart out to her, confessing my biggest fears, and instead of bringing us closer, she seemed to be pushing us further apart. She is shutting down, and I feel helpless against it. I wasn't lying when I told her I was scared. I'm scared shitless. I feel like I'm fighting a battle I can't win. I feel like I'm watching her getting sucked into this world. Something I've been trying so hard to avoid.

I need to do something, change my tactics, so I can stop this. I need to stop this before all is lost. Before my Dove is tainted by Matteo even more.

She is not only pulling away from me mentally but physically as well. Yesterday she spent most of the day in Matteo's personal library, preferring to read a book than spend time with me. This morning after breakfast, she disappeared into the library yet again.

Tired of waiting around for her, I leave the room and head toward the library. Every guard I pass looks up at me, their watchful eyes examine me and my mood.

When I enter the grand room, filled from top to bottom with

books, I find Dove curled up on a chair by the window. A book laying on her lap. Her head snaps up when she notices me walking in. I'm surprised to find her eyes puffy and red like she's been crying.

"What's wrong?" I shoot the two guards posted at the door, an accusing glare. They better not have touched her. "Did someone hurt you?"

"No, come sit." She sniffs. "I need to talk to you."

Hesitantly, I take the seat across from her. I know whatever she is about to tell me is not going to be good. I mentally prepare myself to hear what she has to say, but the truth is, nothing could have prepared me for what she says.

"You need to leave, Zane." A semi-truck could have hit me, and I would feel less wounded. "You can't stay here any longer. This..." She motions between us. "Whatever this is, it's not working. We need to end this now before it gets any further."

"*Any further?*" There is no further. We are already at the end. I've loved her for years, and she loves me back. "We are meant to be together."

"No, we are not. I'm meant to be here. I'm meant to carry on the Castro name, and you don't fit in here, at all." I know she is playing. She doesn't mean this, she can't mean this, but hearing the words come out of her mouth, regardless of their truthfulness, hurts like hell.

"Just stop, Dove! I can't listen to this shit. You and I both know that's not true," I growl. "Drop the act, I don't care who is in the fucking room. Just stop!"

"This isn't an act. I want you to leave, Zane. I need to do this. I need to marry Alberto, and you need to go your own way."

I want to cover my ears with my hands, so I don't have to listen to this or cover her mouth so she can't get another word out. Either way, I can't listen to this any longer.

"I'm not going anywhere," I growl, ready to destroy something. Getting up from my seat, I start pacing around. "And I'm not letting you marry some fuckhead just because some guy tells you to."

Twisting to fully face me, the words that come out of her mouth next cut me straight to the core. "I don't want you, Zane. I don't want to be with you, and the more you push me to do something I don't want to do, the more I'll push back. I want you to leave and not come back. I want you to forget about me and move on. I don't want to be with you. I'm not in love with you." Her expression is skewed, but her eyes tell me she is lying.

"You're lying, you love me. I've protected you your whole life. You need me just as much as I need you."

"I never asked you for any of that. I didn't even know you were there most of that time!" I turn away from her, but she gets up from her seat and gets in front of me, so I have to look at her face. "Maybe I needed you before, but that's because I thought you were all I had. I thought all my family was dead, but my father is alive, and he loves me. I don't need you anymore."

"Shut up," I yell, stepping closer. Close enough to where she has to lift her head to look into my face.

"Just go, Zane. Don't make this even harder than it already is. Just go..."

"I will never leave you. Never!" I grab her upper arm and hold her in front of me. I want to shake some sense into her. I want to make her understand, see how wrong this is.

"Let go of me," Dove demands, her voice on edge, but that only makes me hold onto her tighter. I feel like if I don't, she might disappear forever, slip away, and never return to me.

"Take your hand off of her," one of the guards growls.

Turning to him, I snap, "She is mine, I touch her wherever and however I want."

"I'm not yours!" Dove yells and shrugs out of my hold. Just when I thought this whole situation couldn't get any worse, Dove says something that will haunt me for a very long time. "I don't know how much clearer I can make it. I don't want or need you. I don't love you, and I want you to leave and never come back." Before I can respond, she drives in the final nail. "Guards, please make him leave the house and don't let him come back."

"Dove! You can't be serious?"

She backs away from me, moving out of reach. I try to take a step forward, reaching out my arms to her, but the two guards are already on me, pulling me back. I start to fight them, throwing punches at anything and everything I can reach. More men pile into the library, trying their best to get me under control.

I've lost count of how many men are fighting me, five or six... All I know is that I can't let them win, I can't let this happen. If I leave now, Dove will be all alone. I won't be able to protect her from the outside.

I'm vaguely aware of Dove's voice in the background, asking them not to hurt me. I almost laugh in the midst of all of this. They could throw acid on me, and it wouldn't hurt as bad as the pain she is putting me through herself.

By the time the men have managed to shove me out of the room, my arms are worn out, and my muscles sore. I'm still healing from my last injuries, and I'm not at my strongest, but I can't just give up either. So, I keep fighting them, even when everything hurts, even when my chest aches so much I think it might have cracked wide open. Even then, I keep fighting because right now, that's the only thing I have left.

18

Dove

Zane's face as the guards forced him off the property, still haunts me and it's been days. The despair, the burning rage, and the way he yelled my name, telling me I didn't mean it. I can still feel the sadness. It's suffocating. I carried his heart in my hands. He gave me the one thing he'd never give anyone else, and I took it and crushed it. No matter what I do, I can't forget. I can't unfeel the pain I've caused.

In my father's presence, I play the perfect daughter, a smile painted on my lips at all times. But behind closed doors, within the four walls of my room, I'm a blubbering mess, it's like I've lost a piece of myself by letting him go.

Pressing the heels of my palms into my eyes, I will the tears away. I have to get it together. I have to. There is no other way to do this. It was either let him go or watch him die, and I'd rather have him hate me for a short time, thinking that I really didn't want him, than to never have a future together.

Sucking a sharp breath into my lungs, I nearly jump off the bed when a knock echoes through the room.

Shit! I can't let anyone see me like this. Matteo is expecting it, waiting, watching in the shadows for me to slip up. At the first sign of weakness, he's going to pounce, so it's better not to give him a reason to jump at all. Taking another calm breath, I clear my throat and then speak.

"Yes?"

The knob twists, and the door opens. Laura, one of the maids, pops her head into the room, and I almost sigh in relief. *Thank god.* Since my father found out about me kicking Zane to the curb, he's been pushing Alberto and I together more.

He's even moved the wedding date up, and since I don't plan to marry Alberto, I'll have to make good on the next step in my plan soon.

"Ms. Castro, I'm sorry to interrupt you, but your father wanted me to let you know that the stylist will be here soon to prepare you for the engagement dinner."

"Oh, yes. Thank you, send them up whenever they arrive." I give her a smile, which she returns before slipping out of the room and closing the door quietly. Given my fake breakup with Zane, my emotions have been on edge and my mind, of course, else-where, so much so that I nearly forgot that the engagement party was today.

Matteo invited everyone far and wide and decided that having it here at the house was the best choice. It would give everyone a chance to see how rich and powerful we were. At least, that's what he told me. I agreed mainly because disagreeing wasn't an option. I finally have him on my side and eating right out of the palm of my hand. He's already been more lenient with me. Letting me walk around the house, spend the day in the library, even letting me walk outside in the garden on my own.

I won't mess this up. I didn't hurt Zane for nothing. I did this for him, for us. Now, I just have to figure out how to escape... the wheels in my head start turning. Tonight. I'll make my move tonight. Matteo will be too focused on the guests to notice if I go missing, plus, with all the traffic in and out of this place, I'll have enough of a distraction.

My lips turn up into a sly smile. My heart may be broken, but it won't be forever. I'll make this right.

~

Two hours of hair and makeup later, and I'm finally getting into the strapless red piece that Matteo picked out for today. It's tight and shows off my breasts and slim waist. I can barely breathe in the damn thing. Looking in the mirror at my reflection, I'm tempted to take it off. I hate it, hate it so much because all it's going to do is draw unwanted attention. I don't want everyone staring at me, watching me, whispering about me as I pass by them. My snowy-white skin looks even paler, and though my hair and makeup is pure perfection, the rest of me just looks blah. Then there's the fact that Zane isn't here tonight. I'm lost without him, like a broken compass that doesn't know its way.

All the thoughts swirl and weigh heavily on my shoulders. Grabbing onto the marble counter just to have something to hang onto, I count back from ten in my mind. By the time I reach zero, I'm a sliver less likely to have a full-on mental breakdown. The door to the bedroom creaks open, and I step out of the bathroom just in time to see Matteo walking into my room, his dark hair is slicked back, and the suit he wears clings to his body like a second skin. He looks every bit as evil as I know he is.

"My dear, you look so beautiful." He reaches for my hand and brings it to his lips, pressing a kiss to the skin. I do my best not to tug from his grasp.

"Thank you, you look great as well."

Dropping my hand, he smiles, his eyes twinkling with appreciation. "I wanted to let you know that I'm very proud of you. I didn't think you would do it, but like always, you surprise me."

He's referring to my breakup with Zane. Great, now he wants to talk about it.

"It had to happen, it was him or my obligation to the family, and

I wasn't going to choose some man over you. You're the only family I have, and the last thing I want to be is a disappointment." I bat my eyes for effect and watch as the mask on his face melts away like a chocolate bar sitting on steaming hot pavement.

"You could never disappoint me. You have Castro blood running through your veins. It's not in us to do such a thing." I almost snort at his response but suppress it at the last second, and instead, cover it up with a massive smile.

"Shall we get to the party?" I ask in an overly excited tone.

"We shall." He smiles down at me, and I try not to sink deeper into the uneasiness that's pooling around my feet. As we descend the stairs, people cheer, and I realize then that the festivities have already started. My eyes collide with Alberto's dark ones. He's waiting at the end of the stairs for us. I can see the desire rolling off of him in waves.

He thinks he has a chance, a shot at being with me. He doesn't know shit. My father passes me off to him, and I take his arm in mine, ignoring the churning in my gut that his touch brings. Matteo dismisses me and starts chatting with two men that look to be of some importance.

"You look absolutely divine," Alberto murmurs into the shell of my ear as he guides me through the maze of people. I recognize a few faces from the previous welcome home party, but none of the names from that night stuck, so all over again, I feel lost in a sea of unknown faces. It's even worse this time because Zane isn't here.

My chest tightens at the thought of him, and it feels like someone is using my heart as a damn stress ball.

"Look how excited everyone is to see us together." Alberto tightens his hold on me, almost as if he's trying to show everyone how possessive he is. "I can't wait to make you my wife and solidify our stronghold over the west. No one will think to try and fight us."

I don't dare tell him the only thing he's going to be looking forward to is his death because then that would ruin the surprise. Smiling up at him because there are so many wandering eyes, and I need to continue to play the part, I let him walk me through the double French doors and outside. The garden has been transformed into a party area with a buffet, tables, and chairs.

The space is decorated with fresh cut roses, tea lights, and string lights that hang above the entire area. They twinkle like stars and give the place a more intimate and elegant feel. It's beautiful, breathtaking, and I kind of hate that Matteo put something as great as this together. A man as evil as him, shouldn't be allowed to come up with such beautiful things.

Alberto and I take our seats at the head table, a flute of wine is shoved into my hands, and I take tiny sips of it as I'm forced to endure small talk with my father's guests.

"I can't wait to fuck you raw," Alberto leans over halfway through the dinner and whispers into my ear.

I feel disgust slither through me and all the way to the tips of my toes. This is the worst part of playing this game. Making those around you assume that you care and are interested.

"I can't wait either," I say, placing a hand on his thigh beneath the table. His eyes flash with primal hunger, and I know all I'm doing is taunting the beast inside the cage.

The night drags on and on, and after some time, Alberto disappears, maybe he's screwing someone else, or maybe he's talking with some of Matteo's men. I don't know. I should probably be worried, considering that he's been gone awhile, and this is our engagement party, but I'm not. If anything, I'm thankful for his absence.

It's one less person I have to pretend that I give a fuck to. Some guests linger, but many leave after dinner, which is exactly what I'm planning to do right now. If I'm going to escape, it has to be tonight. Since Matteo is busy smoking cigars and drinking bourbon with his buddies, he won't even realize that I've slipped away.

I'll never get a more perfect moment than this evening. As I glance down at my half-eaten plate of food, my eyes catch on the shiny knife blade. *Weapon.* You need a weapon, Dove, my brain screams. Lifting my eyes, I look around suspiciously to see if anyone is watching me before I grab the knife and tuck it blade side down into the side of my dress, beneath my armpit. No one should see it there, and I'll be able to make it up to the room without incident.

Pushing away from the table, I meander back into the house and toward the grand staircase. My foot has just barely touched the bottom step when a hand wraps around my arm and tugs me backward. Turning to face the owner of said hand, a gasp catches in my throat.

"Where are you going, Ms. Castro?" One of Matteo's guards asks. He's smiling, but his smile doesn't reach his eyes, he looks more like a tiger smiling at its prey.

"To my room. Is that okay, or would you like to interrupt my father and his colleagues to see if he would be okay with that?" I pin him with a glare, trying not to show my fear or trembling lips and tug my arm out of his grasp. His fake smile slips away, and he looks a little mortified, his cheeks turning crimson, probably because he's never been talked to like that by a woman before.

"Go on," he says without another word, and I force myself to walk up the steps, instead of running like I want to. With my heart racing out of my chest, I reach the top step and bound down the hall, almost falling over my own feet in the process. Reaching the door, I twist the knob and push it open. Slipping inside, I close the door, and the darkness of the room surrounds me. I sigh, but that sigh is soon swallowed by an almost scream when the bedroom light comes on, and Alberto's hulking frame comes into view.

"Hello, my soon to be bride," he murmurs. I swallow the fear of being alone with him down and force air into my lungs.

All you're doing is acting... give an Oscar-worthy performance.

Crossing the space between us, I sashay my hips and smile at him while batting my eyes as if I'm interested. I don't know the first thing about being seductive, but I'm pretty sure my attempt is working because Alberto's smile widens as he gets up from the bed.

His jacket has already been removed, the white button up shirt he's wearing is pulled out and wrinkled. His hands move to his dress slacks, undoing his belt, we meet in the middle of the room.

Everything about this feels wrong, but I can't stop now.

"I came up here to tell you that I planned to fuck you tonight, but it looks like you were thinking the same thing I was." The edge of his voice is as sharp as the knife blade I'm hiding in the side of my dress. If I can get close enough, maybe I can stab him without him ever seeing it coming.

"Of course, why don't you help me out of my dress," I purr and twist around, giving him my back. It's a daring move, one that could be dangerous if I'm not careful.

"It'd be my honor," he growls, his hot whiskey breath fans over the back of my neck, and I shiver with fear knowing that it's all or nothing now. I'm either going to end up on my back, making the biggest mistake of my life, or with blood on my hands.

His fingers grip the tiny zipper at my side and start to tug down. At the same time, I drop the tiny little clutch I was holding in my hands to the floor as a distraction.

As I had hoped, Alberto leans down to grab it, and that's when I make my move. Pulling out the knife, I grip the handle in my clammy hand and twist around to face him just as he's coming to stand at his full height.

I don't think, all I do is act as I swing the blade through the air, and diagonally across his throat. Blood sprays like a water sprinkler from his neck, and the lustful haze in his eyes slowly turns to panic. He reaches for me, but I take a step back, bumping against the edge of the bed. Dropping the knife, it lands on the floor, and a second later, so does Alberto.

Adrenaline rushes through my veins, and all I can do is stare, my hands shaking, watching as the life drains out of him.

I killed someone. Something must be wrong with me because I don't feel anything, not a single thing. Actually, I take that back, I feel relieved, free, a bird that's going to escape her golden cage. An idea pops into my head, and I step over his body and start to go through his pockets. Keys jingle inside his dress pants. *Bingo.* Fishing them out, I stare at the key fob to his car. That's my ticket out of this place. They'll never think twice if I drive out of here in his car.

I pick up the knife from the floor and take it into the bathroom with me. I put the knife down long enough to strip out of my blood-soaked dress. Then I pick the knife back up and get in the shower. Holding on to the smooth silver handle of the steak knife while standing under the spray, I watch as the water turns from red to pink, and then clear.

When I'm clean of all the blood, I get out of the shower, dry off and hurry back into my room. I pull on a pair of leggings, sports bra, T-shirt, and a pair of tennis shoes.

Tucking the knife into the waistband of my leggings, I go to the bedroom door. Opening it a crack, I listen for anyone that may be close by, especially guards. Matteo may have lessened them in the days since Zane left, but there is still a heavy presence, especially tonight.

Stepping into the hall, I lock the door and close it firmly behind me. It's now or never. At the end of the hall is a laundry shoot that leads into the laundry room, which is just off the maids' quarters. I know this because I had accidentally walked down there one day while checking out the mansion. Opening the wooden door that hides the shoot, I look down into the dark tunnel.

My heart clatters in my chest, but I know I have to do this. Climbing into the shoot, I grip the edge of the door, my fingers biting into the wood a second before I let go. I can't breathe, can't see, and all I want to do is scream as I slide through the dark on my belly.

All too soon, the ride is over, and I land in a heap of clothes and sheets, the air expelling from my chest upon landing.

I can't believe I just did that.

Climbing out of the pile, I scurry to my feet and look around the room for the nearest exit. When I spot the door and walk to it, all I can do is hope and pray that it's unlocked. I reach for the brass doorknob and wrap my fingers around the cold metal. My heart pounding out of my chest in anticipation. It turns, and I push the door open. I sigh in relief when the brisk fresh air blows through my hair.

For a few seconds, I just stand there, breathing in and calming myself before I poke my head out carefully. Looking left and right, I don't see any guards. I slowly walk outside and close the door behind me. Almost... I've almost made it.

With the key heavy in my pocket, I sneak around the house, staying as close to the wall and in the shadows as I can. Most cars are parked on the lawn in the front yard, and that is where I'm heading.

When I get to the edge of the makeshift parking lot, I take out the key fob and hit the unlock button. Like a beacon in the dark, headlights start to flash a few rows down, and I weave through the cars to get to them.

I climb into the luxury car and push the key into the ignition with a shaking hand. It turns, and the car roars to life. I buckle up quickly before putting the car in drive and pulling out of the spot.

Heading for the main gate, I let possible scenarios of the next ten minutes run through my mind. If everything goes according to plan, the guards will just wave me through, thinking that I'm Alberto. If they see that it's not him and try to stop me, I will hit the gas and hope for the best. Worst case scenario, they shoot at the car and kill me... I don't want to think about that. No, that's not going to happen. I will make it out of here.

I approach the gate, and as hoped, as soon as they see the car, one of them motions to open the gate. It isn't until I'm only a few feet away that he can look into the windshield and realize that it's not Alberto driving the car.

Pushing my foot down all the way, the engine revs up, and the car jolts to the front. Both guards pull their guns just as I speed past them. I hear the shots; I feel something hitting the car, but I keep driving. My eyes are wide open, I don't think I even blinked the last few minutes. My blood pumps through my veins furiously as the car accelerates even further. I look down at the speedometer, which reads ninety-eight miles per hour. This is the fastest I've ever driven, but it's still not fast enough.

Looking in the rearview mirror, I don't see anyone following me yet. I caught them by surprise. Good. That gives me a head start. I have no doubt that they will come after me.

I don't take my foot off the pedal. All I can think about is getting away.

I will get away. I will be free, and I will be back in Zane's arms.

19

Zane

Looking up, I squint my eyes at the bright neon letters reading *Nightshift*. I don't know how exactly I ended up here, or why I'm here at all. Sure as hell, isn't because of the naked women dancing on the stage. Even after Dove ripped my heart out and trampled it, she is still the only one for me. I can't even think of another woman.

Maybe because it's the only place I know I can keep drinking without getting jumped by Christian's guys. They wouldn't dare set a foot into Damon Rossi's strip club.

My head is swimming, my mind clouded from the enormous amount of alcohol I've already consumed. Still, I want more. I want to drown myself in it just to make the pain go away.

Stepping inside, the smell of cigars, expensive liquor, and cheap perfume hits me. I'm barely inside when a half-naked woman greets me with fuck me eyes and pouty lips.

"Not interested," I slur, brushing her off before pushing past her. She says something, but I ignore her, heading straight to the bar instead. I take a seat and wave the waitress over. Quickly, I realize that I saw her last time I was here.

"Here to see Damon again?" she yells over the music.

"Not today. Just pour me a whiskey."

"Whiskey coming right up," she chirps, way to happily for my taste. It's almost like she enjoys working here. *Who the fuck likes working in a strip club?*

A few moments later, I have a large glass of amber liquid shoved in front of me. I murmur a thanks before I grab the glass and bring it to my libs. Taking a huge gulp, I let the alcohol burn down my throat, enjoying the way the warmth spreads out through my insides when it settles in my stomach.

My vision is already blurry as I look around. My gaze catches on two men on the other side of the bar. They're watching one of the strippers doing her dance routine on stage with hungry eyes. A little bit too hungry for an innocent show like this.

When the song is over, and the girl walks off the stage after collecting her money off the ground, the two guys look like they're about to jump her. She gives them a smile as she walks by, and that seems to be enough of an invite for them to grab her and pull her between them.

Even with the music blaring over the speakers loudly, I can hear her squeal in surprise, followed by her asking them to let her go. Her resistance doesn't seem to bother either of the guys, since they just move in closer, caging her in between their bodies.

Slamming my glass against the countertop, I get off my seat and walk around the L-shaped bar quickly. Grabbing the first guy by the back of the neck, I pull him off the girl. He tries to twist in my hold while swinging at me, but I've already got my arm around his neck, holding him in a chokehold.

Before I can get this guy unconscious, his friend grabs the bar stool and lifts it in the air, swinging it at my head. Normally, I could have seen that move coming from a mile away, but in my current state, everything is fucked up.

I'm fucked up...

The hardwood lands with a crack against the side of my head that's so hard, I'm surprised I don't black out right then. I do, however, see stars. Releasing the guy, I stumble back and try to gather my bearings, but before I can do that, I'm being hit again, this time a meaty fist cuts across my face.

A woman's scream pierces my ears as fists of fury rain down on me, clobbering every inch of my face. Pain is a welcomed feeling though. It blends with the pain that Dove caused me. I'm so gone now, I don't think I could even bring my arms up to protect my face even if I wanted to. All I can do now is exist at this moment, and let the pain rule my life. The light inside my head flickers in and out, and I know it's coming.

One more punch and the light goes out.

Darkness surrounds me, but I welcome it.

Only in my dreams can I be beside Dove again.

∼

WHEN I COME to it feels like I've been hit by a truck before sliding down the side of a mountain face first. My face is throbbing so much so, I swear I can feel my heartbeat in the side of my head.

What the fuck happened?

The memories flicker through my mind like an old movie reel with some scenes missing, the film ripped apart. Dove... drinking... the bar... a fight. Either, I drank way more than I thought, or I got hit in the head pretty hard. On second thought, I'm sure it's a combination of those two.

I pry my eyes open slowly, immediately thankful that there is not much light in this room. Blinking, I try to make sense of where I am. The room is bare, brick walls surround me, and it doesn't take long for me to realize I'm in a cell.

Fucking hell.

Sitting up, I'm forced to close my eyes yet again, as the entire room starts spinning. When I open my eyes this time, I see the iron bars, confirming that, indeed, I'm in a cell. There is nothing inside but a cot that is creaking beneath me with every move.

I look around the cell, scanning every inch before I get up. The only thing I find is a water bottle sitting next to my cot. I grab it, unscrew the cap and start drinking. My parched mouth welcomes the cool water. I don't stop until the entire bottle is gone. Still, I feel more thirst. Damn, I'm dehydrated. Of course, that's the least of my worries right now.

My first thought is Christian found me, but he would have probably killed me right away. Castro is my second thought, but why would he want me locked up? No, both of them would have either killed me right away, or I would have woken up to being tortured.

I push myself up to stand on unsteady feet. Swaying slightly, I walk to the iron bars so I can look up and down the hallway. At the far end, I see a man posted. As soon as he catches sight of me, he turns and starts to walk away from me.

"Hey, asshole!" I yell after him. Instead of getting a reaction out of him, I make my ears hurt. The sound echoes through the hallway, only intensifying my headache. *Ugh.*

Walking back to my cot, I sit down and try to gather my thoughts. Where the fuck am I, and how did I get here? Most importantly, how the hell will I get out of here?

A few minutes later, I hear someone approaching. Getting myself ready for a fight, I get up on my feet and let my hands form fists beside me. Every muscle in my body is tense when I see none other than Xander Rossi appear on the other side of the cell door.

"Good morning, Zane. Sobered up enough to behave?"

I'm so shocked at seeing him, that I'm speechless, but I'm even more shocked when he reaches in his pocket and fishes out a key to unlock the cell door. The door swings open, and he takes a step to the side, motioning for me to come out.

"Is this a joke?" I say, my voice raspy like I smoked a pack of cigarettes last night.

"Not at all. Let's go, we have a lot to discuss."

Hesitantly, I walk past him while anticipating an attack any moment now. He has to be joking. What could he possibly want with me? If he thinks I have some dirt on Christian or Matteo, he's going to be wildly disappointed.

He makes me walk ahead of him, down the hallway and up a flight of stairs. When we get to a second hallway, and I don't know which way to turn, he takes the lead and lets me walk behind him. I don't miss that huge display of trust, him turning his back on me like that. He's showing me that he trusts me, probably expecting me to trust him in return. The question is, why?

I'm shocked yet again when we turn the corner and go through another door. Looking around confused, I wonder if I'm still sleeping, and this is a dream because now I'm standing in a foyer of a mansion... I assume the Rossi mansion.

"Why am I here?"

"Let's go sit down. I had my cook prepare some breakfast for you. I'll explain everything while you eat."

He leads me through the house and into a huge dining room. As he said, an array of breakfast food is spread out on the table. Part of me wants to refuse the food. I still don't trust him, I have no reason to, but given my current state, sustenance will greatly benefit me.

We both take a seat. Xander pours himself a coffee, and the smell of freshly brewed coffee invades my senses. He pours me a cup as well, without asking if I even want one.

"Talk," I order while taking up a fork and start eating the omelet in front of me.

I glance over at Xander, who is raising an eyebrow at me, clearly surprised by my lack of fear of him. After a moment, he starts talking anyway.

"As soon as I saw Dove, I couldn't believe the resemblance she had to someone I know. I figured they had to be related in some way. I started digging when she was here, but I hit one dead end after the next. After I let Dove go, I kept looking. There was something about her that I was missing, and I couldn't let it go."

Where the fuck is he going with this story?

He pauses to grab something from the inside of his suit jacket and places it in front of me. My gaze falls onto the old photograph, and for a split second, I think it's Dove looking back at me, but I quickly realize that the woman in the picture is a little bit older than Dove, her hair just a little bit lighter and her lips just a tad bit less full.

"Who is that?"

"My mother," Xander says, and I almost drop my fork. "My first thought was that Dove had to be my mother's daughter, but when Dove told me her age, it became an impossible scenario. Dove is twenty-one, and my mother died twenty-two years ago... or so we thought."

"What do you mean?" I almost don't want to ask. If Dove is not only related to Castro but also to Rossi, she'll be forever caught between the two families.

"Like I said, I couldn't let it go. So, after Dove left, I took her toothbrush and had her DNA tested, matched against mine. The test results confirmed that Dove is my sister."

"Wow..." I don't really know what else to say to that. "So... what does that mean for Dove?" *From the frying pan into the fryer?* Fuck, she will never be able to live a normal life.

"It means that I'm going to help you get her away from Castro. We're going to take him down and protect her at all costs. She is my family, and I protect what's mine."

At least one thing we can agree one.

20

Dove

I can't believe that worked. I'm free at last, and I did it all on my own. Matteo's men never caught up to me. I had too much of a head start. It takes forever for my heart to return to a steady beat and even longer for me to stop peering over my shoulder.

For the last couple hours or so, I've been driving around without a destination in mind, too focused on simply getting away. Now that I'm certain I've lost them, I need to find a place to go, and I need to find Zane. But how?

He doesn't have a phone. I have no idea where he is staying or how I could get a hold of him. I could go back to the bunker if only I had a clue as to where it is. *Shit.* I hit the steering wheel with my hand. I should have thought of this before, but I was so busy playing the role of an obedient daughter that I didn't think my plan through to the end.

The only place I can think to go is my apartment. Maybe he still checks the surveillance there? It's a small chance, but that's all I've got right now. At the very least, I can go and leave a note for him and hope that maybe that's where he goes, once news breaks out that I escaped.

Taking the next turn, I drive deeper into the city, taking the long way to my apartment. I'm still on high alert, looking into the rearview mirror constantly, and scanning my surroundings for threats the entire time.

When my apartment building finally comes into view, a mixture of relief and fear washes over me. What if he had the same idea? Maybe he left me a note, or maybe, just maybe he is there waiting for me? I can only hope. I park two blocks down, not wanting to leave the car in front of my building. It'll draw attention, and that's the last thing I need right.

Getting out of the car, I walk down the sidewalk with my hand on my waistband, where the knife is hidden underneath. When I get to the front door, I raise my hand to ring my neighbor's doorbell, hoping that someone is still awake and will let me in. But before I can push the small round button, the door flies open.

I reach for my knife, ready to protect myself, but quickly realize that it's only the couple from the floor above me.

"Oh, hi," Susan greets me in surprise "We were worried about you."

"Nothing to worry about." I force a smile. "I'm fine just staying with a friend."

"I'm sorry about the break-in," James, her husband, says, "we called the cops when we heard the commotion downstairs, but when they got here, the burglars were already gone."

"I'm just glad I wasn't home," I say, my tone honest.

"Well, let us know if you need anything. We're heading out for a late-night pizza run."

"Thank you, I will." We say our goodbyes, and I move past them and into the hallway. Walking up to the apartment, my hands shake. When I reach the door, I find that it's slightly ajar. It's probably been that way since Christian's men came and kicked it in. *Assholes.* I wonder if they found my stash of cash, or if they were too concerned about finding me to care? Probably the latter. Guess we're about to find out.

The door creaks as I push it open, and my mouth pops open as I take in the chaos that is my apartment. Every single item is flipped over, all my belongings tossed around the room like an f-5 tornado went through it.

It's just belongings... I tell myself as I step over pieces of broken furniture. I killed someone today. I can handle seeing my apartment ransacked.

Closing the door behind me, I ignore the destruction beneath my feet and walk into the bathroom. I have to focus on the now. What I need to survive, to find Zane. Which leads me to the entire reason I came back here. *Money.*

Opening the medicine cabinet, I scan the bottles, which, surprisingly, haven't been touched. Finding the bottle I'm looking for, I pop the cap, and smile when I see the cash rolled together inside. I used to laugh whenever I'd hide money in here, thinking how ludicrous this was, but look who's laughing now. Sliding my fingers inside, I tug the money out and squeeze it in my clammy hand. I drop the bottle into the sink and close the cabinet.

I don't want to stay anywhere too long right now, not with just having escaped Matteo. Leaving the bathroom, I walk to the bedroom, my shoes crunching against the floor. The room is destroyed just like the rest of the house, but I make do, finding some clothes and a backpack to shove them in. Tossing everything inside, I sling the pack over my shoulder and walk out. In the kitchen, I find an envelope from a bill on the floor and a pen sitting on the counter.

Part of me had hoped like hell that Zane would be here when I walked through the door, but he wasn't, and that's okay. I'll find him, and we will be reunited again. On the off chance, he does happen to stop by here, I write a note, letting him know I've escaped and that I'll come back here in a few days. Leaving the note on the counter, I walk to the door.

I should probably get rid of the car. Now that I have some cash, I can take the bus or a cab. I start walking down the sidewalk with every intention of passing Alberto's car, but when I spot two black

SUVs coming around the corner, I freeze. Yes, it's just an SUV, but it's the speed that it's coming around the corner. Danger zings through the air, and my gut tells me to run.

The first SUV speeds up, and now I'm certain whoever is driving is coming from me. Springing into action, I rush around the car while unlocking it with the key fob. As fast as I can, I slide into the driver's seat and start the car. The engine roars to life, and I'm barely able to pull out of the parking spot before they're catching up with me.

The street is filled with the sounds of tires squealing and cars speeding away. Driving like a Nascar driver, I punch the gas, zooming away from them. Every fiber in my body tenses when I look in the rearview mirror and see that they're right on my tail.

They could be Matteo's men, or Christian's. The least scariest possibility is that they're Xander's, I couldn't see them chasing after me though, not like these cars are. Turning down an alleyway, I drive through two trash cans and make a sharp left back out onto a street. Headlights flash behind me, and I know they're still there.

Slamming on the gas, I weave through traffic, nearly hitting three cars in the process as I try to get away from them. If they catch me, I'm trapped. It doesn't matter whose men they are. I'll be a pawn on one of their chess boards when all I want is to be free. Taking another sharp left, I peer over my shoulder and see only one SUV.

Where did the other... The thought gets lodged in my head and scatters like puzzle pieces shoved off a table when out of nowhere, the second SUV comes barreling down a side street. Its headlights are blinding, and I squint, trying to figure out what they're doing. It only takes a second to realize they're heading straight for me. The nose of their car slams into the rear of mine. My teeth clatter together as the impact sends the car into a tailspin.

Tires squeal, and headlights flash in front of the car, making me dizzy. All I can think is to run. With sweaty palms, I reach for the door handle and shove it open. I don't think about where I'm going, only that I have to get away.

My lungs burn and my heart thunders in my chest. It's almost the only thing I hear as I dash from the car and out into the street. Crazed, I pause for one second and look over my shoulder just as the sound of car doors opening meets my ears.

"Get the girl, but don't kill her. I want to be the one to do that."

I know that voice. *Christian.* Shit. I didn't escape one crazy-ass mob family to be tossed into another. Forcing my feet to move, I start running down the sidewalk. I make it all of ten feet before a muscled body plows me into the ground with the force of a wrecking ball. The air expels from my lungs, and my hands scrape against the concrete as I try and break my fall. Twisting in the assholes grasp, I drag my nails down and across his face. A hiss passes his lips, but he doesn't release me.

"Feisty. I like it." The bastard sinks his fingers into my skin with bruising force. "Keep fighting me. I love it when they do." The weight of his body disappears, and just when I think I might have a chance of escaping, he yanks me up off the cold ground and starts dragging me back toward the cars.

"No, please...please, let me go," I resort to begging because I know what happens if I get shoved into one of those cars.

"I got her boss," the bastard dragging me behind him announces proudly. In a few steps, we're at the SUV. The door opens, and no matter how much I struggle against the hulk of a man, I'm picked up and placed into the backseat of the vehicle, beside one of the most villainous men I've ever met, next to Matteo.

The door is slammed shut, and it feels like I'm being encased in my own coffin.

"We meet again," Christian says, his voice drips with anger, rage that is suffocating. It's like trying to breathe underwater.

"Let me go," I order. Like a cat, I claw at the door of the SUV, tugging at the handle, but the door won't open. The vehicle starts to move, and no matter how much I will myself not to cry, I can't hold back the avalanche of tears.

"Why would I do that when I just got you back?"

"So, you gonna put me in a cell again?"

"No, Dove, you're coming with me to my place this time. I'll let you stay in my room if you behave." He smirks, and I have to force the bile rising in my throat back down.

"What do you want from me? I have nothing of yours... Zane is... we aren't together, and I don't know where he is, and Matteo wants me dead if you think he cares about me, you're wrong." I look up at the man through thick lashes, tears clinging, no matter how hard I try to blink them away.

A sadistic grin pulls at his lips. "That's the problem, Dove. You think you have nothing, but really you have everything, and by the end of this, I'll take it all from you."

Confusion seeps into my pores, but before I can try and piece anything together, Christian produces a needle and stabs it into the side of my neck, pressing the syringe down and injecting me with some unknown drug.

"Night, night, little bird, when you wake up, all will be different."

21

Zane

"**I**f you keep pacing like that, you're gonna leave scuff marks on my carpet," Xander growls from his desk, annoyance lacing his words. That makes two of us. I've had enough of mob bosses telling me what to do.

"If your men would hurry up and find her, I wouldn't have a reason to pace." I pin him with a stare that's sure to get me killed. I still don't trust Xander, and I'm not sure what his real intentions are, but right now, he is helping me, so I need to really rein in my anger.

"They'll find her," he snaps before returning his attention back to his laptop. I have no doubt that they will find her, but I fear that it's going to be too late by the time they do, and I don't want to imagine the condition she'll be in by then.

"I just can't wait around any longer. I'm going to go look for her myself."

"I already told you, it's best to stay here until we know what's going on. My informant gave me too little information to act right now," Xander explains again as if I didn't hear him the first ten times. Apparently, Xander managed to get one of Matteo's men on his payroll. That guy called an hour ago, saying that there was an incident at the mansion. Alberto is dead, and Dove has disappeared. Whether she escaped or was taken is still not clear.

Fuck, I hope she escaped. If not, I'm burning down the world until I find her.

"At least check the surveillance in Dove's apartment again. If she got away, she would go there, I know it."

"It's still pulled up on my computer. If she goes there—" He pauses mid-sentence, his eyes fixed on the computer screen. "She just walked in..."

I'm across the room and around Xander's desk in two seconds flat. My eyes fall onto the computer screen and catch sight of Dove... my Dove, walking into her ransacked apartment. Through the grainy screen, she doesn't appear to be hurt or really even frightened. In fact, she looks strong, like a queen. Her gaze scans the ground, looking over her destroyed belongings before moving up and right into the camera. She doesn't know where I hid the cameras, but somehow, she manages to look straight into it.

It's like she's staring at me, beckoning me to come for her.

I'm coming, baby...

"Ivan and his team are outside and ready to go. I'll stay here and continue checking surveillance. Go!" Xander commands, and for once, I have no problem taking his order.

Without saying a word, I'm out of his office and running toward the front door. I almost take the handle off while opening it. When I make it to the front steps, I realize Xander wasn't lying. Ivan is standing in front of a fleet of cars, seemingly only waiting for me to get in. He doesn't have to wait long, because the next instant, I'm shoving into the passenger seat.

Ivan jogs around to the driver's seat, and we are off before either of us can buckle up.

The ride to her apartment seems to take forever, even though Ivan seems to have his foot to the pedal most of the drive, it still feels like forever. Even if we were going a thousand miles per hour, it wouldn't be fast enough when it comes to Dove.

"She just left the apartment," Xander says over the car speaker.

"We're almost there," Ivan says as if he knows how anxious I'm feeling. Grinding my teeth, I hope and pray that we'll catch her before she leaves. These last couple of days have been pure torture, and even if I am angry at her for pushing me away, I still want to hold her in my arms just to know that she is okay.

A few minutes later, we pull up outside her apartment. I open the door and jump out of the car before we come to a complete stop. Looking around, I wish nothing more than to see her. I scan the entire area, up and down the street, but she's nowhere in sight... gone.

She's gone.

I fucking missed her.

⁓

LOOKING DOWN at the envelope in my hand, I read over the note for the hundredth time.

ZANE, I escaped Matteo. Will be back in a few days.

I LOVE YOU, Dove.

REFUSING to return to Xander's place, I meander back outside, I sit in the car and wait. I told Ivan he could leave, but he insisted on staying, mumbling something about how I might need him. Two more SUVs stayed as well, parked only a few spots behind us. I look out onto the street, watching every car that drives by and every person that walks out onto the street.

If I have to, I'll stay here until she shows back up. Either way, I'm not moving until we figure out where the hell she is.

Xander has been trying to figure out where she went, calling in favors left and right while we wait around uselessly. When the phone finally rings, and Xander's name flashes over the screen, I almost give up hope that he has some new information and is instead ordering us to return to the mansion, but that's not what comes out of his mouth.

"Christian has her. There was some type of chase, and now they're transporting her to his place. I'm sending more men your way, but it's going to be a good twenty minutes before they get there, and I'm not sure she has that long."

"We're going there now," Ivan says as the SUV roars to life. I clench my hands into tight fists at the thought of a fight. Why is he taking her to his place? What the fuck is going on?

My heart beats in my ears, and all I can think about is rearranging Christian's face, and wrapping my arms around Dove. Making sure she's safe and secure. Clenching my jaw, I try not to think about what might be happening to her. I can't believe this is happening again. I should have killed him when I had the chance. If they've hurt her in any way, they'll be wishing for death by the time I'm done with them.

"I'm guessing you know where to go?"

"Yes, head east." I continue giving Ivan directions until we arrive at Christian's private mansion. It's not as heavily guarded as Xander's place, but it does have its own security. Luckily, I know that security system well, and if I'm lucky, he was stupid enough not to change my code to get in.

"Is there a back way in?" Ivan asks.

"No, but you can pull up to the gate and try to enter my code. It's 891384."

Ivan drives up to the code pad and punches in the numbers. I hold my breath as he pushes the enter button, and I don't breathe until the green light blinks, and the gate starts to creak open. I suck in a ragged breath as Ivan drives through the gate and toward the house.

"I can't believe he didn't change the code." Ivan shakes his head.

I snort and say, "I can. He's too confident, and that's exactly what's going to get him killed... tonight." I half expect Ivan to tell me not to do it, that Xander wants to bring him in and torture him, but to my surprise, he only nods as if he was expecting me to say that.

"Xander told me to kill him if you didn't want to do it in front of Dove. I know you don't trust him yet, but I can tell you, he's nothing like Matteo. He actually loves his family, and now that Dove is a part of that, he'll spare her any type of pain that he can," Ivan says as we pull up in front of the mansion.

"Then let's go inside, get her, and kill the bastard who's trying to hurt her," I say while opening my door with my gun in my hand.

As soon as we're out of the car, a handful of Christian's men pour out of the house, guns raised. I stay close to the car, using it as a shield while I raise my own gun and start shooting. The first bullet hits my target right between the eyes, his body crumbling to the ground. The second one hits another guy in the arm, but Ivan gets him in the side of the head without even blinking. The other two men retreat into the house but fail to close the door. *Idiots.* Not that a closed door is going to stop me from getting to Dove. I'll rip this fucking place down to the floorboards to find her.

More shots are fired, some by us, some by Christian's men, but everybody is keeping themselves covered. I know I need to act fast; I don't have time for a fucking standoff with these idiots. Taking the risk because a bullet to the chest is nothing compared to the pain Dove will endure if we wait any longer, I push off the car and spring up to the front of the house. A guard sticks his head out the door in a failed attempt to survey the area. Without thinking twice, I lift my gun and pull the trigger while running toward him.

He falls back against the door and then crumbles down to the ground just as I get to the door. The last guard lunges for me, fear trickling into his features as if he knows the fate he's about to be delivered. Expecting it, I greet him with a punch to the chest, knocking the air from his lungs. A gasp slips from his lips, and before he can recover, I press the muzzle of my gun to his stomach and pull the trigger. Like a tiger, I move through the foyer and toward the kitchen.

A scream pierces the air and bounces off the walls of the house, and like a beacon, I'm drawn to it. Dove needs me, she fucking needs me, and I'll be damned if I fail her again. Turning, I walk back toward the hall, where I hear a whimper instead of a scream this time. I'll rip his heart out of his chest if he hurts her.

Uncontrolled, and like an animal hunting its prey, I move deeper into the hall. I can sense Ivan behind me, his movements mimic mine, but he doesn't intervene or try and stop me.

"Time to go, princess." Christian's smug voice pierces through the heavy fog around my head, and I hide slip into the room, hiding behind the door. When I peer back around the corner, Christian is tugging Dove down the hall with him. I only catch a glimpse of her face; her cheeks are stained with tears. "Your little knight thought he could save you, but all he did was damn you. You should thank me for killing you and putting you out of your misery."

Dove's cries are muffled, but I can feel her pain, taste her fear on the tip of my tongue. I have to stop them before they get to an exit and get outside. Christian wasn't prepared for us to show up here, and so we have the element of surprise right now, but I'm sure he's called more men in, and they'll be here soon.

Too bad Christian will be dead before that happens. Tiptoeing in the direction he went, I lift my gun, watching as he tugs Dove by her arm toward a door. She struggles in his grasp, and as she fights him, her gaze swings toward me. Panic. Fear. Adoration. Love. Each emotion reflects back at me.

Shaking my head, I release myself from her trance. The door opens, and I lift my gun, firing two shots into Christian's back.

I don't think, I pounce like a thief in the night, rushing toward them. Christian releases Dove at the last second, and before I can grasp what is taking place, he shoves her toward the open door. Fear like I've never felt before, pulses through me with its own heartbeat as I watch her disappear into the dark space. I hear every stair she hits, my heart cracking inside my chest, and as Christian turns to face me, a sadistic smile on his lips and a gun in his hand, I lift my own and shoot him in the head at point-blank range.

Shock flickers in his eyes, and then blood and brain matter explode everywhere, painting the hall in death. Christian's stare becomes vacant and reflects back at me. He crumbles to the ground, landing in a heap at my feet. I step over his body and rush down the stairs, my hands shaking, and my body vibrating with fear as I reach Dove.

She is lying on her side, her arms cradling her head. I kneel next to her on the floor, not sure if I should pick her up or if that would hurt her more. I gently grab her arms and pull them away from her face, so I can get a better look at her. Brushing the sweat-slicked hair from her face, her eyes flutter open and find mine in an instant.

"Are you okay?" I ask, my voice raw with emotion.

"My head hurts, but I'm okay... are you? Are you okay?" Her eyes move over the front of my shirt before she reaches for me, her hands fisting the material in her hands.

"I'm fine, sweetheart," I murmur against her forehead as I pluck her off the floor and cradle her frail body in my arms. I'm not sure what kind of injuries she has, but I need to get her out of here. More of Christian's men could arrive at any second, and I'm not going to fall into that trap. Racing up the steps, I meet Ivan's dark stare at the top.

"Is she okay?" he asks gruffly, his eyes flicking over her face.

"I don't know. He shoved her down the stairs, and she's complaining that her head hurts. She's not bleeding, but I need to get her to Xander's and have the doctor check her over before I can be sure."

Ivan nods, and I walk out of the house, carrying the woman I'd die a million times over for. No one will ever hurt her again, not while I'm still breathing.

22

Dove

W ho knew that your life could fall apart and come back together so fast in one day? Zane pulls me tight to his side and kisses the side of my face. I feel his heartbeat in his lips.

Taste the fear in the air. His arms are like steel bars wrapped around me, and I've never been happier in my life to be confined to a space, because I know I'm the safest I'll ever be while in his arms. A shiver rips through me, and goosebumps pebble my flesh. This could've been really bad, terribly bad, but because of Zane, Ivan, and the rest of Xander's men, I'm safe. I don't know what Zane had to do to get Xander and Ivan to help us, but right now, I don't care enough to ask. I'm sure I'll find out sooner rather than later.

Everything is going to be okay now.

I've survived Christian and escaped Matteo; the worst is behind us.

"I'm pissed at you for forcing me to leave you unprotected. If anything happened to you, I wouldn't have been able to forgive myself," Zane growls into my ear like an animal, crushing me to his chest.

"I'm okay. No one hurt me," I reassure, shifting in his arms, so

I'm facing him. I cling to him like a second skin, letting the warmth of his body seep into mine.

"You took a pretty good tumble down the stairs. That's not nothing, and the only reason it wasn't worse than that is because we got to you in time. Imagine if we had been five minutes later?" Zane's fear has never been so real to me. I always knew he was worried, but I'd never seen real fear on his face for me until tonight when he rescued me.

"I know... I know, but you weren't, and I'm okay. Everything is okay. I love you, and I'm sorry, so sorry." Tears fill my eyes and slip down my cheeks. Zane wipes them away with his thumb, and I stare up at him through blurred vision, waiting for him to say something.

I won't ever tell him, but I was so afraid, afraid that I would never see him again, never get to tell him how sorry I was for pushing him away, for trying to save us both.

"I accept your apology, Dove, but we aren't done talking about this, not by a long shot. I could've lost you today, and I know what you did was to protect me, but it's my job to protect you. My job," he snarls, and I feel his anger, his fear rolling off of him and slamming into me. "Did anyone touch you? Alberto? Christian?"

"No one touched me. I wouldn't let them." Burying my face in his shirt, I inhale his unique scent of soap, and manliness, trying to calm myself. *I'm alive. I'm safe.* I repeat the same words over and over again to myself. Zane holds me so tightly it's hard to breathe, but I wouldn't trade it for the world.

I stay like this cradled in his arms, my head against his chest, the sound of his heartbeat in my ear until the SUV comes to a rolling stop. Lifting my head, I discover we've been brought to Xander's mansion.

All I can do is hold my breath and wait for something bad to happen. It's a battle of mobs at this rate, and Zane and I are the only two pawns left on the chessboard.

The doors to the SUV open, and I slide across the leather seat with Zane at my back, his hand wrapped around my wrist like he's afraid I'll run away or something.

Coming to stand outside the vehicle, I marvel at the huge wooden door before us. It's massive and intimidating, just like Xander Rossi. I suppose I shouldn't expect any less from such a man. Zane tugs me to his side, giving me a look that I can't quite read.

The door creaks loudly as it opens, and Xander's impassive face comes into view. Instead of looking at me like I'm a bug he needs to squish, he gives me a warm smile, it's almost cheery if you could picture a man who kills people for a living being jolly. It actually looks more like a shark smiling at you with all of its pointy teeth on display.

"Welcome home, baby sister."

The air in my lungs stills, and I'm positive my ears have deceived me. He didn't just say that, right? *Sister?* He has to be on drugs or something.

"Ssss-sister?" I barely get the single word past my lips.

"Yes. Come in, please, have a drink, sit down, and we can talk. You've had a tiring day, Dove, and I don't want to exhaust you further. The doctor is already on his way to check you over, but while we wait for him, we can talk."

My mouth refuses to work. Whatever words I'd prepared myself to say, sink deep into the back of my mind. Zane holds me tightly to his side as he gives Xander a weary look before guiding us into the mansion.

This has to be a trap. No way am I this man's sister. I don't have to know all that he's done to know that he's a man of power and evil. He might have treated me nice while I was here, but I've heard enough stories. He's the head of a notorious and ruthless crime family, after all. It's not like he's Santa Claus.

Zane guides me into the house and through the massive foyer, and I'm in awe of the beauty of the house. Ella isn't just a sweet person but also has excellent taste in decorations.

I try not to think about how fucked up that is as Zane moves us into a small seating area off the dining room. There's a floor to ceiling bookshelf on one side of the room and a leather sofa and two chairs centered around a small wooden table on the other. Two huge windows make the room feel bigger than it is.

Zane navigates us to the sofa while Xander takes the chair across from us.

"Would you like anything to drink?" Xander asks.

"Water," I croak. I'm not sure what's going on. He called me his sister, but that can't be right. Matteo never talked about me having any other siblings.

Xander disappears from the room and returns with a glass of water a moment later. He hands it to me, and I take a sip before placing it on the table in front of me.

"I'm sure you have a lot of questions, but I'll tell you what I know first, and then you can ask me anything that you want to okay?" Though Xander's voice still toes the line on menacing, there is a softness to it.

"When Ivan brought you here last time, you looked so familiar to me, but in a way that didn't make sense. You looked a lot like my mother, and I couldn't figure out why. I asked your age for a reason. My mother supposedly died twenty-two years ago, so when you told me you were twenty-one, I didn't think it could be true. Still, something in my gut told me to keep digging, thinking we might be related in a different way. Distant cousins at the very least. Instead, I found out that our mother didn't die when I thought she did. She left when she discovered she was pregnant with you."

I try to swallow, but the salvia in my mouth feels like concrete. A sense of Deja vu sets in. I've been here before, rescued from Christian, then being told I have some long-lost relatives. It didn't work out for me last time, so no surprise that I'm not happy about this new development. For now, I keep my thoughts to myself and listen instead of speaking.

"Our mother had you without any prenatal care, and by

herself. There is no record of you ever being born, and you were never given a birth certificate. Police found you in a hotel room crying when you were about two, our mother dead from a drug overdose."

My hand tightens in Zane's, and I feel like I'm going to be sick. I have two brothers, maybe more I haven't met yet. All of them seem to be part of the mafia. On top of that, I have a father who is part of the mafia but not the same family.

My mother had an affair, ran away, and gave birth to me, god knows where, before deciding, later on, it was too hard to love and care for me. At this point, I truly do feel as broken as I look. Unwanted and unloved. It's the story of my life.

I don't even realize I'm crying until I feel the wetness against my cheeks. I look from the ground and over to Zane, hoping he didn't know. He knows everything about me, surely, he knew about this. Still, a tiny piece of me hopes he didn't know. When our eyes clash, I know instantly that he did, and like a plane, I nosedive right into the ground.

"I didn't know until a few days ago," Zane whispers, trying to reassure me. It's like I'm being cornered, all my fears and worries bombarding me at once.

"There's more," Xander says in a monotone voice.

"What more could there be?" I whisper though I had hoped the words would come out stronger. I feel weak and broken inside. It's strange because I knew most of the story. It's harsh to know I spent my entire life in foster care when I had family, a family that is wealthy, and that I could've been living with. Even if they are ruthless criminals, family is family, right?

"After you left, I sent your toothbrush in for a DNA sample. You just looked too similar to my mother for me to let it go. The test result confirmed my suspicions, that we are related but even more shocking, turns out you aren't just our half-sister, but our full-blooded sister..." Red hot rage pulses through my veins in an instant.

"So, wait... both of your parents are my parents? Which means..."

"Matteo was lying to you the whole time," Xander says before I can. "You are not related to him."

"Why would he lie to me?" I growl, asking no one in particular. "Not that I am disappointed about having no connection to him." Matter of fact, I'm a little relieved.

"Because he's a fucking prick," Zane replies.

"Actually, he might not have known he was lying. I think our mother did have an affair with him, but she was pregnant at the time, so he doesn't know you're not his daughter. He assumed, and since our mother was trying to escape our father, it makes sense."

I'm sinking in all the secrets I've been told, drowning a slow and painful death. I start to shiver, my thoughts swirl as I think of all the things I did, how I betrayed Zane. Yes, I did it to save him, but I didn't have to butter up to Matteo. I didn't have to... guilt makes my chest cave in. I can't breathe. I try and suck air into my lungs, but it feels like I'm choking.

"This is a lot to take in," I whisper just as the sound of a knock fills the room. Everyone looks up to the door, where a man with a stethoscope around his neck and a bag in his hand stands.

"Ah, Doc, please, come in," Xander greets, and the doctor steps in. "I need you to check her out. Make sure she is fine," he orders.

The doctor nods and approaches me. For the next few minutes, he gives me a good checkup. Feeling for breaks, taking my vitals, and asking me a bunch of questions, all under the watchful eyes of Zane and Xander.

At the end, he tells me what I expected. Besides a bump on my head and a few bruises on my body, I'm fine. He leaves a few minutes later, and I am once more alone with Zane and my brand new brother.

The doctor was a brief distraction, but now I'm hit with the reality of my new life once more.

"Can you give us a little bit," Zane says, turning me in his arms.

Xander nods and walks out of the room. As soon as he's gone, Zane pulls me onto his lap and wraps his arms around me. He holds all my broken pieces together, holds me together.

"I'm sorry. I'm so sorry, Zane," I sob into his shirt, feeling so torn and tattered.

"Don't be sorry, baby... You did what you thought was right, and that's how we both made it out of that situation alive. Matteo will pay for deceiving us, pay for trying to rip us apart. Pay for hurting you. You're mine, Dove. Mine to protect, to cherish, to keep. Mine until I breathe my last breath."

"I'm just confused. I don't know what to think, what to feel. First Matteo tells me I'm his daughter, now I'm suddenly Xander's sister... I just don't know how to take any of this."

"Let's go upstairs so we can talk."

Pulling away, I look him in the eyes, those dark eyes of his still give nothing away, but I know deep in their depths there is love and adoration for me that can never be rivaled by another.

"I'm sorry I hurt you... I never meant to push you away. Matteo told me if I didn't get you to leave, he would kill you, and I couldn't let you die." More tears fall, blurring my vision completely now, and I know I'm on the verge of a full-fledged panic attack.

"Shhh, you can make it up to me. Like I told you, Dove. I will never leave you. You could stab me in the heart, shoot me in the head, lie, or cheat, and I still wouldn't leave. Your crazy matches my crazy, and I'm never going to give you up."

His confession only makes me sob harder, and even if I wanted to, I couldn't object as he picks me up like I weigh nothing and carries me back out into the foyer and up a grand staircase. My vision is too blurry to make anything out, but I tell myself I can check out my surroundings tomorrow.

Zane opens a door and walks inside, closing it behind him with his foot. He deposits me onto the bed and takes the spot beside me.

"Now, let me hold you. I miss the way you smell and the way you feel in my arms. I need you like an addict needs their next fix,

Dove, and I'm not sure I'm strong enough to deny myself what I want from you right now. So, please, roll over and stop looking at me like I'm a knight when really I'm the devil waiting to crack you open and feast on your soul."

"You're not the devil, Zane. You're the sun, and the moon, and every star in my galaxy. Without you, there would be no me. I'm sorry I hurt you. I'm sorry all of this happened." I know I already apologized, but I feel like I need to say it a few more times for it to sink in.

I roll away from him, wondering if he can see the shame and sadness in my face. Wrapping an arm around my middle, he holds me possessively, like there is no way to escape him, not like I would try anymore.

"I just want a normal life..." I whisper, more to myself.

His lips trail against the back of my neck, and I shiver in his arms.

"Normal will come, my sweet, Dove. But not until we paint the city red and take over Matteo's empire. Now sleep, you'll need it for what I have prepared for you."

"What's that?" I murmur half asleep.

"You'll see, tomorrow. I need to remind you who you belong to." A tiny shiver of excitement runs through me as I remember the last time he showed me that I'm his. I remember how good he made me feel, how he tied me down and made my body sing. How he coaxed orgasm after orgasm out of me.

I need this. Need him. All of him.

The dark and the light, the good and the bad. I need it all. I need his body against mine. Need his darkness like I need my next breath. If there is anything I've learned from this last month, it's that the only constant in my life has been Zane. My stalker, and me, his obsession.

23

Zane

A knock sounds against the door, and I roll over with a groan, remembering that Dove is still hurt. The doctor assured me that she had nothing but a little bump on her head. He gave me some pain pills to give her but said that she was lucky to walk away with nothing more than a bump. Rolling out of bed, I tug on a pair of boxers from the floor and walk over to the door. Opening it, I'm greeted by Ivan's emotionless face. The dude reminds me more of myself every day.

"Xander wants you and Dove to meet him downstairs for a meeting, whenever you are ready. Damon is here too," he says and then turns around and walks back down the stairs.

Closing the door, I turn my attention back to Dove. She is curled up in the bed, looking broken. The last few weeks have taken a toll on her. Her wings clipped. Her beautiful face puffy from all the tears she shed last night.

She'll learn to fly again soon, but it won't be without me by her side. Rage and lust swirl together and burn like a raging inferno through my veins. I want to punish her. No. *I need to.* I need to remind her that she belongs to me and that it's us together or nothing.

Reaching for her, I stroke her face gently like she's made of the finest glass. She stretches like a kitten, lifting her arms above her head. Her blue eyes open, and I'm struck by their beauty. My obsession, my unwilling captive. She's forever tied to me. Cupping her cheek, I lean in until our lips are almost touching. I allow myself to feel every emotion that I've repressed in the last couple of weeks. Hate. Anger. Pain. Betrayal.

My touch is gentle, even though it shouldn't be. I could never hurt Dove, no matter what she did to me. I could never hurt her as she's hurt me.

"I want you to know that even though I love you, I want to hurt you. I want to make you bleed the way you made my heart bleed when you forced me to leave you with Matteo," I say, my voice quivering with emotion. I'd never been angrier and scared all at once. The memory of her forcing me to leave, telling the guards to toss me out is all I can see in my mind.

I was scared shitless for days, worried sick knowing that if something happened to her within the walls of that mansion, there was nothing I could do. I was forced to leave her unprotected, and I wouldn't ever do that again.

Shocked by my confession, Dove's pretty mouth pops open. I know she's been through so much, everything she endured and discovered about her history. I know I should let her heal, give her more time, but I can't stop myself from punishing her. Physically hurting her isn't an option, but there are worse ways to make someone feel the pain they've inflicted on you.

"I want you naked and spread out for me."

Understanding blankets her face, and her pink tongues dart out, wetting her bottom lip. I want to taste her lips, bite, and suck on them, but I can't. Not yet. Pulling my hand away, I watch as she slowly slips out of her clothes, a cami, and pair of cotton panties, discarding them on the floor. My eyes roam over the length of her body, looking for any inflictions, cuts, wounds. Aside from a few bruises on her arms, I see nothing that worries me.

Pressing a hand to her chest, I gently push her back onto the mattress. She doesn't say anything but watches me like a timid mouse that's been caught in a trap. Pushing her legs apart, I drag my gaze lower, over her tiny tummy, and her hips before reaching the top of her mound.

Her creamy smooth thighs come into view, and I bite back a groan. They're unblemished, and as I lean in, I inhale her sweet scent into my nostrils.

The smell of her sex zings right through me and into my cock, slamming into me like a lightning bolt. Like a dog with a bone, I'm salivating, wanting to take a bite out of her pink pussy. *One taste. One lick. One drop of her sweet nectar on my tongue.*

That's all I need, but because I know I'll take more, so much more than that, I rein myself in. Using every ounce of discipline I have left, I pull away.

"Do you have any idea how much it hurt me to be pushed away by you? To watch you do as Matteo said, to hang on his every word." I pause and trail a finger down over her thigh, stopping at her knee. She shivers, and I'm unsure if it's from fear or something more. I hate that I enjoy her fear, hate that it makes my cock harder than steel. "I watched you play with Alberto, taunting him, leading him astray..."

"I didn't... I wouldn't. I'm sorry," she eventually huffs.

My lips turn up at the sides, "No, you aren't. Not yet, but you will be soon."

"What are you going to do to me?" she asks after a second, her heart beating against her ribs like a bird trapped in a cage.

"Whatever I want," I reply darkly. I'm too frenzied with need to prepare her, and so I hope like hell she's already wet because the last thing I want to do is hurt her, then again, she hurt me. Ripped my fucking heart out of my chest. Granted, she did it to protect me, this I understand, but who protects her if something happens to me?

"Zane," she whimpers, knowing what's coming. I'll be cruel to her, but I'll make sure she feels my love with each hard stroke. I'll give her pain and let the pleasure soothe the ache.

"Shh, you only speak if it's to tell me to stop. Do you understand?" I bark out.

Her gaze widens with shock and arousal, but she doesn't object. Instead, she nods her head in understanding.

"Play with your tits, get yourself nice and wet because I don't have the patience for that right now."

Dove's chest starts to rise and fall rapidly, but her eyes glaze over with lust. She likes when I tell her what to do, when I fuck her with purpose. Rolling her hardened nipples between her thumb and pointer finger, her lips part and her hips roll, seeking out my cock. I leave her this way, craving and wanting for a minute while I watch. She bites her bottom lip to stifle the whimper, trying to escape her pouty lips. I want my cock between those lips. I want to watch her swallow my length, to choke on it, to be so helpless and fragile.

Shoving my boxers down, I let my swollen cock free and kick away the fabric at my feet.

"Come here," I order, fisting my cock in my hand. Dove's timid gaze moves from my cock and up my body, stopping at my eyes. "I want you on your knees," I say.

Grabbing a pillow from the bed, I toss it on the floor at my feet. Dove's movements are sluggish, and I can see how aroused she is for me, her sweet cream coats the insides of her thighs, and my gaze is drawn to it.

I want to lick it, feast on her, to wring every drop of pleasure out of her.

This isn't about her... I remind myself, which is really fucking hard when the only thing I care about is her. Pleasing her. Making sure she's safe. Loving her. I breathe for her.

Dove sinks down onto the pillow and eyes me cautiously.

"Open that pretty mouth of yours. The same mouth that slayed me with such hateful words. I'm going to fuck it, fuck your mouth, throat, and then your pussy." I've never been so blunt with her before, so vile, but it feels good. It makes me feel free. I'm not sure what I'll do if she objects, but thankfully, she doesn't.

I bring the tip of my cock to her open lips. She flicks her tongue against the tip, and I let out a grunt. Fuck, that feels like heaven. Running my fingers through her hair, I stroke her head before sinking my fingers deep into the dark strands, wrapping them around my fist. I tug her head back and make sure she knows who's in charge.

"Open your mouth real wide, I'm going to fuck it."

It's the only warning I give her before I thrust my hips forward, shoving my cock deep into her mouth. Her tiny nails sink into my thighs, and she whimpers around my length. Pulling out a little, I slam back in and watch as her eyes water and the tears stream down the side of her face. Again, I hold myself there for a moment before pulling back out and doing it all over again. She gags around my length, and the sound only heightens my pleasure.

"You look so fucking pretty with my cock stuffed in your mouth," I say, wanting her to know that while I am punishing her, I still love her so fucking much.

Dove's mouth is so warm, so fucking perfect. I pull out again, and saliva dribbles out the sides of her mouth. I half expected her to tell me to stop by now, but Dove is stronger now than she was back in that bunker. She's a queen.

Moaning around my cock, I swear the sound goes straight through me. Repeating the process again, I continue fucking her mouth until the pleasure in my balls becomes too much, and I'm afraid I'll blow. I'm going to fill up her tight little pussy with my come.

Pulling all the way out of her, I grab her by the chin and stare into her crystal blues.

"Get on the bed on your hands and knees," I order, and she scurries from the floor and onto the bed. Climbing onto the bed, I situate myself behind her, pressing down on the small of her back.

She's at the perfect angle, her pink folds glisten in the morning light.

"You come when I tell you to," I growl and line up my cock with her entrance. Thrusting my hips forward, I slip deep inside of her channel, my home. She's snug, tightly squeezing me like a vice.

"So deep," she pants into the sheets, and I slap her ass hard for talking outside the rules.

"Don't talk unless it's to tell me to stop."

Those are the last words I say for a while as I fuck her hard and fast, showing her just how much it hurt me to lose her. Imprinting my soul on hers, I fuck her like an animal, rutting deep. Every time she gets close to orgasming, I pull out. She whimpers at the loss, and when I push back into her, we repeat it all over again.

"Zane," she pleads, and it's the one time I let her get away with talking.

The need in her voice is too much for me. I can feel her gripping me, her tight cunt getting ready to pulse around me. I've been fucking her for ten minutes now, beads of sweat drip down my body, my grip on her hips is bruising, the force of my thrusts harsh, but I can't seem to get enough of her. I can't seem to get her to feel all of my pain. Withholding her orgasm is killing me as badly as it's killing her.

"Please, Zane, please. I'm sorry. I'm sorry..." She starts to sob, like actual crying, and it's the last shred. I can't take hurting either of us anymore. Slamming hard into her one last time, I grind my hips against her ass, feeling everything as she explodes all around me. We both come together, my hot come fills her channel, and I can feel it dripping down my cock and onto my balls.

Fuck, I've never come so much or so hard before.

Gently, I pull out of Dove and collapse onto the mattress beside her. I tug her into my side and stroke her sweaty face with my hand. It takes me forever to catch my breath, but when I do, I roll, so we are facing each other.

"Was I too rough?" I ask a tinge of guilt in my voice.

"No. I'll be sore, but you taught your lesson." The little smile she gives me is enough to make the guilt disappear.

"I love you, Dove. I love you so fucking much, and no one is going to come between us again. I'll kill anyone who tries, anyone who even thinks about it. You're mine, and I am yours. Say it," I urge, needing to hear her say the words.

"I am yours," she whispers, and I've never heard truer words in my life.

24

Dove

I feel the way Zane fucked me in every step I take, and I'm pretty sure that was his intention. I took away his power when I forced him to leave, and I needed to show him that I placed that control back into his hands. I know he needed this as much as I needed it myself.

The way he used me was terrifying. Like I was nothing to him, but at the same time, invigorating because, in the end, I held all the power. If I told him to stop, he would have. I could feel his anger slipping away, the pain crumbling little by little.

After lying in bed for a few minutes, we get into the shower together, where Zane takes his time helping me wash my hair and body. His hands are gentle as he moves the washcloth over my skin and down between my legs. I gasp at the contact; my folds still sensitive.

Zane's expression fills with concern. "Are you sure I didn't hurt you?"

"I'm sure. I'm just really sensitive." I give him a sincere smile, and we finish together in the shower without any more worrying questions. As soon as we're done, Zane gets out, grabs a towel, and wraps it around me. It's fluffy and smells clean and fresh.

Slinging a towel around his own waist, we walk back into the bedroom together. I sit on the edge of the bed while Zane walks over to the dresser and starts rifling through it. I can't help but stare as his well-defined muscles clench and flex as he moves.

Those perfectly sculpted abs and the bulge of his biceps cause a heat to coil low in my belly. I shouldn't be staring. I really shouldn't, but...

"Xander's wife gave me some clothes for you to wear if you want to come and look through the drawers," Zane says, his voice interrupting my thoughts. My cheeks heat, and I can't imagine how I look right now.

"Oh, okay, yeah..." I mumble and walk over to the dresser. I find some clothes and pull them on, feeling a little less exposed now that I'm dressed. Drying my hair with the towel, Zane watches me curiously.

"You know what happens next, right?" he asks, as I drop the towel to the floor.

"Yes, now that Christian is dead, Matteo is next."

"Are you okay with that?"

My brow furrows. "Why wouldn't I be? I told you, I don't care about him, Zane. I was only playing along to protect you. He told me he'd kill you if I didn't make you disappear, and so I decided I'd rather have you angry with me than never have a chance to see you alive again. Who will protect me if you're not here?" I whisper as I cross the space between us and cup his cheeks. I lean in and press my lips against his.

They're warm and firm, and when I feel his tongue pressing against the seam of my lips, I open up to him. Our tongues duel for a short while, each stroke of his tongue, stoking the warm coil of pleasure inside my belly. I know Xander is waiting for us, but he can wait a few more minutes.

Zane's hands circle my waist and he tugs me forward...I'm seconds away from ditching my clothes and climbing on top of him when a knock on the door interrupts us.

Of course, Zane pulls away with a groan, a tiny smug grin pulling at his lips.

"We should probably go. I think we've left your brothers waiting long enough."

My brothers. It's so strange to think that yesterday I had no siblings, and today I have two brothers. Giving my hips a gentle squeeze, Zane moves me out of the way so he can get to the door. Tugging it open, I'm shocked to see Xander standing on the other side.

"Sorry to interrupt your reunion, but we need to discuss Matteo as soon as possible. Now that Christian is dead, word will travel fast."

"We'll be down in a minute," Zane confirms, and Xander nods.

Sticking to his word, we walk downstairs and into the massive dining room, where Xander, Damon, and Ivan are sitting. They're talking casually like they aren't plotting to murder someone tomorrow.

It's hard not to outright gawk at all the fancy features, like the huge open kitchen off to the right of the dining room, or the chandelier with ten thousand shiny diamonds reflecting back at me. Zane takes a seat at the table, and I take the spot next to him. A maid pops her head out of the kitchen and meanders over to us with a kind smile.

"Can I get you anything?" she asks.

"No, I can get it..." I start, but Xander clears his throat, cutting me off.

"That's not how this works, Dove. The help is here to help. That's what we pay them for. If you want something to drink or eat, Matilda can get it for you." His words are clipped and cold.

I feel like a small child who's being scolded, and I'm reminded of my stay at Matteo's mansion, and I dislike greatly that he called this lovely woman *the help*.

"I'll just have a coffee. Cream and sugar, please," I say through gritted teeth before taking a seat. Zane takes the one next to me and slides his hand over mine.

"The Sergio family is crumbling apart without Christian, and Castro is running around like a chicken with his head cut off, trying to take over whatever territory he can. Greedy bastard he is. Plus, Alberto being dead leaves him spread thin. Now is the perfect time to strike, to take him down once and for all," Xander explains while Damon and Ivan nod in agreement.

"Matteo tried to marry me off and threatened to kill Zane if I didn't do his bidding. I'm all for taking him down as fast as possible."

"Good, because we might need your help—"

"Whoa, whoa," Zane interjects. "You are not involving her in this! This was not part of the agreement. I told you I would help, but we never talked about her."

"I won't force her if she doesn't want to. I'm simply offering her the chance to help."

"She declines," Zane growls without even asking for my opinion. "She doesn't belong here in this world, and she's definitely not going anywhere near Matteo again."

"Let me ask you a question," Xander says cunningly, a sinister smile spreading out across his face. "What exactly happened to Alberto? How did you escape Matteo?"

"It doesn't matter," Zane snaps, and I just now realize that he hasn't asked yet and that I haven't told anyone either. Does Zane know I killed him? Does Xander suspect it? He must, he wouldn't have said anything, otherwise.

"You've been awfully quiet, Dove," Damon says. Speaking for the first time, a hint of amusement in his voice now. He looks identical to Xander but maybe a bit younger, and just a tiny bit less scarry.

"I... I killed Alberto," I blurt out. All eyes fall on me. Xander and Damon seem prideful, while Zane is shocked, his mouth hanging open.

"You killed him?" I watch his Adam's apple bob as he swallows. Something in my chest swells. "Yes. I found him in my room during the engagement party, he wanted sex, I didn't. So, I slit his throat before stealing his car keys and making my escape to the apartment. I waited a little while, stole his keys, and escaped and went to my apartment." A tinge of guilt echoes through me. "I'm sorry, I didn't tell you. You never asked, and well, we never got the chance to talk about it."

"See, she's not as weak as she seems." Xander pins Zane with a glare, crossing his arms over his chest. "In fact, she's more of a Rossi than I expected her to be."

For some stupid reason, I smile.

"That doesn't mean she is going to run headfirst into danger right after I get her out of the crossfires," Zane yells. "You are not forcing her into this like Matteo did."

Xander's gaze turns murderous, and his hands curl into tight fists on the table. "Don't compare me to him," he says in a tone that has the small hairs on my neck standing on end. "I already told you, it's her choice." He turns to me. "If you want to leave, you are more than welcome to walk away right now. I won't hold it against you, and if you ever need anything, I will be here for you. I am simply giving you the opportunity to help."

"I'll help; however, I can. If you need me to do something, I will. I'm not afraid."

"The hell you will." Zane slams his fist down on the table, making the glasses jump.

"If she wants to help, then she can. We wouldn't let anything happen to her. I get your concern, but she escaped without you, she can handle this." Damon says this time, and I know even without looking at Zane that he's pissed, a vibrating wall of rage. I understand his fear, his anger, but I don't want to be seen as a delicate little flower. I saved myself once, and I'll do it again, except this time, I'll have an army of men beside me.

"What's the plan?" Ivan questions his eyes on Xander.

Xander rubs at his chin. "We use Dove to draw him out. Make him think that she's coming back to him, or better yet, put her out in the open. Make him think that she's unprotected. Then before he gets her, we end him."

"Basically, we just fool him," Ivan says.

"Basically," Damon replies. "It's really simple and safe, and nothing will happen to Dove. She is family, our sister. That fucker won't get his hands on her again." Damon's words are directed at Zane, who is still silently sulking beside me.

"When are we going to do this?" I ask.

"Tomorrow. That'll give us time to come up with a detailed plan. I have a few men tailing him now. We'll place Dove somewhere he can find her and pull her out before anything happens." Xander smiles and slaps a hand on the table. Ivan grunts, Damon nods, and Zane grabs my hand and pushes away from the table.

He practically drags me back up to our room. The door slams shut behind us, and Zane twists around and punches the heavy wood.

"What the fuck happened to you wanting a normal life? He gave you a way out! All you had to do was tell him, no, and we could be on our fucking way out of here. We could leave this all behind us. Ride off into the sunset, happy and together." Pausing for a moment, he shakes his head before muttering, "What were you thinking?"

Anger surges through me, but there is also understanding. I get why he's upset. He just got me back, and now I'm putting myself in harm's way again, but I can't let Matteo slip through our fingers.

"I was thinking that I'm tired of feeling weak and helpless. I want to take Matteo down. He hurt you, hurt us, and I want to make him pay for that." My words stun him into silence, and then I see the anger drain from his body. He sighs deeply, almost as if he is defeated by my response. Then he's on me, his lips pressing against mine, his hands in my hair. He's kissing me like he hates me, like he loves me. Like I'm his reason to live.

Then in an instant, he's pulling away, his forehead comes to rest against mine, and he peers deeply into my eyes. This moment is so intimate, so precious, I almost hold my breath.

"I almost lost you once. The thought of losing you again..." Zane's hot breath fans against my face. "I don't want to risk it. If he were to get to you. If he did hurt you..." The fear in his eyes ripples through me. I can feel it, taste it. It's real, beyond real, and it makes my knees buckle. Zane afraid is terrifying.

"Nothing... nothing is going to happen to me. I trust Xander, and Damon. I trust Ivan, but above all, I trust you. I trust that you won't let anything happen."

"I can't... I can't be sure, and that kills me. It rips me apart. If you die... When Christian shoved you down the stairs..." He exhales. "You don't understand... if you die... I die. There is no me without you."

Snaking my arms around his neck, I tug him closer. "There is no me without you, Zane, and tomorrow we will get Matteo and be free of this cage. We will be free to do whatever we want. I have you to protect me, and you've never let me down."

The look in Zane's eyes tells me he doesn't believe me, but that's okay... I believe, and that's all that matters.

"I'm afraid, so fucking scared, Dove."

"Don't be. I'm not going anywhere."

25

Zane

"I don't like this," I growl into the room as I walk back and forth along the wall. We're all staying away from the window as a precaution. We snuck into the building early this morning before the first filters of sunlight showed in the sky. Our hopes were that no one would suspect us being here. Matteo needs to assume that Dove is here alone.

"So you mentioned," Xander says, his voice laced with annoyance. "She's going to be fine. Ivan is shadowing her. She'll be here any minute."

"She better be. If that door doesn't open in the next ten minutes, I'm leaving..." I barely get the words out when the sound of a key being inserted in the lock fills the room. The doorknob turns, and the door swings open.

I suck in a ragged breath of relief when I see Dove stepping into her apartment. She's beaming, a megawatt smile on her face. "I told you I would be fine."

"This isn't over yet, Dove. You making it here was only half the battle. You are not safe yet," I grumble before pulling her into my arms. She buries her face in the crook of my neck, inhaling while wrapping her slender arms around my waist.

"Just stop worrying," she mumbles.

"I'll stop worrying when Matteo is dead." And that's the truth. As soon as I see the life drain from Matteo's eyes, I'll be free of the fear that strangles my heart when it comes to Dove.

"Now we wait," Damon says as he sinks down onto Dove's couch. I get the feeling he's the most impatient of the two brothers.

We get comfortable on the love seat while Xander sits next to his brother. For a while, we just sit there in an uncomfortable silence. Dove cuddles into my side and plays with the hem of my shirt, either because she is nervous or bored. Honestly, I don't know which one it is, and I don't really care. I just want Matteo to get here so we can end the fucker's life, and I can take Dove back to Xander's.

"Is there any food in this place?" Damon groans as he stretches.

"Can't go five minutes without eating?" Xander scoffs, and Damon scowls at him. For a minute, I'm taken aback by how normal these two seem. Apart from the expensive suits they are wearing, they act like nothing more than two bickering brothers. For the first time, I could actually imagine Dove being their family.

I let that thought run through my head, testing out different scenarios. I've spent the last few days with Xander, and I have to admit, he is not what I expected. He is feared by the other families for being ruthless, and I have no doubt that he is when he has to be, but within his inner circle, he is different than both Christian and Matteo. He treats his family, including the women, with respect, which is unheard of in our world.

"Fine, I'll starve to death, I guess," Damon grumbles, and Dove starts giggling.

"I can find something for you to eat," she says and starts to get up.

"Don't fall for his whining," Xander quips. "He is just being a drama queen. Sit," he orders. "I'd rather you tell us more about you. Like how you grew up, for example."

Dove falls back into the cushion and sighs deeply. I know she doesn't want to talk about that time of her life since it was shitty before she was adopted by Donna.

"I didn't have much of a childhood," say says, shrugging. "I was bounced from one foster home to the next. None of which were great, but I guess it could have been worse. Then Zane and I got put in the same home. That's how we met. The guy hurt him, beat him up badly, and then he tried to hurt me... but Zane wouldn't let it happen." She pauses and looks up at me, her eyes filled with tears, adoration, and love.

"After that, Donna adopted me, and she was great. She showed me what a loving home felt like. We didn't have much money, but it was enough. I definitely didn't grow up like you in a mansion..." I don't think she meant it in a condescending way, but maybe she is just a tad jealous.

"Believe me, Dove. You didn't miss anything growing up at our *mansion,*" Xander says, emphasizing the last word.

"I'm sorry, I didn't mean it like that."

"It's fine. I just don't want you to think you would've had a better life growing up with us because I can assure you that you wouldn't have. Our father was a sadistic prick, and our mother was a helpless victim who couldn't protect herself or her children. Leaving with you, even though you weren't given much of a life, was the kindest thing she could've done." The corners of his mouth tug up into a ghost of a smile. And even though it is a tiny gesture, it's genuine, and I believe him.

"You're right. I wouldn't be half the person I am today if it weren't for my upbringing. Still, it would have been nice growing up with brothers."

Both Damon and Xander look away, their faces fall almost as if they are ashamed of something. I don't understand their expressions until Xander opens his mouth to explain.

"I'm going to be honest with you, Dove. Until I found Ella, I wasn't much different from our father." He sucks in a ragged breath.

"There's a reason the other families fear me. I've always had a reputation of being cruel and ruthless, and that reputation was earned in ways I'm not proud of. There is blood on my hands, lots of it, and though the blood can be washed away, I'll never forget the things that I've done." Regret clings to each word he says, and I understand what he's feeling, the emotions rolling through him. It's because of Dove that I didn't fall off the edge, that I didn't let go completely.

"I'm sure you just did what you had to—"

"No!" Xander cuts her off. "Don't try to sugarcoat it. I hurt and killed people for fun. I wasn't any better than him. Even Damon didn't talk to me for years. Trust me, you can be glad we didn't meet until now. You wouldn't have liked the brother you discovered then."

Of course, I heard the rumors about Xander Rossi, I just didn't realize how much truth they held or how much he had changed.

"I'm still glad I found you," Dove exclaims. "Well, I guess you found me."

"We're glad we found you too. Family is everything to us," Damon interjects. "And now you're part of it."

"I'm not gonna lie, I was scared of you guys, since you know... you basically kidnapped and held me prisoner. Honestly, I still don't know how I feel about everything. I don't know much about you yet, but I hope, maybe we can get to know each other. If you really do want me to be part of your family."

"We do, and you already are part of the family," Damon points out.

Family. The word resonates within me. I never considered having a family with Dove, my obsession with her has always been enough for me. I'm not sure I could ever share her, even with a child of our own, but I know someday, Dove will want kids, and all that matters to me is making her happy. Seeing her smile and laugh.

I want to replace all the bad in her life with good because she deserves it. The day I met her, the kindness she showed me without even knowing who I was or how I got my injuries. It speaks volumes about the person she is. She's an angel, sent from heaven to rescue me.

Xander's phone buzzes, interrupting the moment. "We've got movement outside, two SUV's, blacked out," he says, reading from the screen, then shoves off the chair. His eyes darkening as he adjusts his suit. "It's showtime, boys."

I nod and unglue myself from Dove. I place my hand in hers and pull her to a standing position. I'm nervous as hell about this, but I know Dove can handle it. She's strong, and plus, I'm only a few feet away. Matteo won't even have a chance to touch her.

"I love you," she whispers, wrapping her arms around my middle, "everything is going to be fine. This ends today." When she pulls away, I feel like I'm letting go of a piece of my heart.

Everything is going to be okay... I tell myself as I move into place. Xander and Damon take their spots closest to the door, and I hide in the kitchen. Dove remains standing in the center of the living room. She gives me a reassuring smile, but I won't trust that she's okay until Matteo is dead at my feet.

Silence blankets the room. I pull my gun, preparing to shoot if needs be. The plan is for Dove to lure Matteo into the living room. We'll deal with his men, but the person we want most is him. My heart beats into my throat. There's a knock at the door. Loud and booming.

My gaze flashes between the door and Dove.

God, please... I've never prayed for everything to go right in my life, but I'm praying to whatever god there is above right now that this goes just as planned.

Dove walks to the door, places her hand on the brass knob, but doesn't turn yet. "Who is it?" she asks.

"It's your father. Open up. We need to talk," he demands, his gruff voice filters through the thick wood. "Open up before I kick the door in."

"Are you here to hurt me?"

"*Hurt you?* I've never been prouder. You killed one of my most feared men, escaped my men as well as Christian's. You impressed me, Dove. You are truly my daughter. Now, open up so we can talk about your future like civilized people."

I know he is full of shit, but that's all part of the plan. Dove turns the doorknob and pulls the door open. She backs up into the room, and Matteo steps in, gun in hand.

"You stupid fucking bitch," he growls, pointing his gun at her chest.

Everything happens so fast. I lunge at Dove while Xander and Damon lunge at Matteo, taking him by surprise. A gun goes off, the deafening sound echoes through the small apartment, and my heart comes to a dead standstill.

The next moment, my body crashes into Dove's much smaller one. I tackle her down to the ground, protecting her with my body and hoping that she wasn't hit. Another gunshot goes off, and my ears ring from the sound.

I tilt my head to look at Xander and Damon to find them pushing off the ground while Matteo's body remains motionless on the floor.

"Is she okay?" Xander asks. I shift my weight off Dove to get a look at her. She turns her head and opens her eyes, glancing around with a franticness that matches my own.

"I'm okay. Is he...?"

"Yes, he is dead," Damon confirms. "We need to get out of here before more of his men show up. We just declared war with another family."

"And I'd do it again to protect my family." Xander smiles. I look down at Matteo's lifeless body. It's not how I wanted him to die, but at least he's dead. I wanted to draw things out, make him feel every ounce of pain he made me feel.

"You okay?" Dove's voice pulls me out of the rabbit hole I'm headed down.

"I'm fine. Just glad he's gone."

"Me too," she whispers. I walk us out of her apartment, thankful that the only person that died today was the person who we intended to kill.

26

Dove

After dinner, we retreat upstairs to our room. Zane is quiet, as am I. Once we're alone, the door, closed and locked behind us, he's on me. His lips find mine in a punishing kiss, it's teeth and biting, and his fingers sink into my hair, tugging, needing me closer, needing to become one with me. I fist his T-shirt in my hands, feeling the same intense heat forming between our bodies. There are too many pieces of fabric between us.

We're both panting, our chests rising and falling rapidly. I know he's not done with me yet, not by a long shot. Pulling away, I stare deeply into a pair of brown eyes that are my world. I wish I knew what he was thinking.

Loving Zane is like watching your heart beat outside your body. It's dangerous, consuming, and frightening. It's knowing that at any moment, the one thing you hold dearest could be taken from you. I've endured so much; we've endured so much.

"I need you, Dove. Naked, on your back with your beautiful legs spread wide, showing me that pretty pussy." Each word drips with desire and has my insides turning to mush while sending a zing of red-hot heat down my spine.

When it comes to sex, I'll never tire of listening to him tell me what to do. It turns me on more to be ordered around, to be at his mercy. Following his orders, I tug off my clothes as fast as I can while also trying to look sexy as I do it. Which is harder than it looks.

As soon as I'm naked, I crawl onto the bed, arching my back to give him a view of my pink slit. A deep groan fills the room, and I smile, knowing how much he too wants this.

Rolling over, I lie down on my back against the mattress and let my legs fall apart, spreading them wide, just as he asked. Zane takes his time taking his clothes off, and I enjoy every minute of it. There's something different about this moment, something special. I feel free as if there isn't any weight or fear resting on my shoulders.

My thoughts take a nosedive and become lustful when Zane's cock comes into view. I bite my lip, muffling a moan as I stare at the hard rod in all its glory. It's thick with veins wrapped all around it. He strokes himself a couple of times, and I salivate at the pre-come that beads the tip.

"You want my cock?" Zane asks, crawling up onto the bed. Parting my lips, I go to answer him, but he leans into me and nips at my bottom lip, making me groan. "Is that a yes?" He smiles against my mouth, and I kind of want to punch him, but kind of want to kiss him.

"I don't want it. I *need* it." I emphasize the need because it really does feel like a need. My core is throbbing, pulsing with a heat that I know only Zane can satiate. I'm wet enough that he could fuck me right now, but the dark look in his eyes tells me I'm in for anything but a quick pounding. No, he's going to savior me, drink me like a fine wine, devour me from the inside out. Pulling back, he stares down at me.

"It's time for me to worship your body the way a queen's body should be worshiped."

I plan to ask him in what way he's going to do that, but the words stick to the roof of my mouth when he drops to his stomach between my legs and grips me by the ass, bringing my pussy to his face. Hot breath fans against my center, and I push up onto my elbows, hungry for a view of this man feasting on me.

Which doesn't last long when he starts licking my clit like it's an ice cream cone. I slide my fingers through his hair, tugging at the soft strands, urging him forward. Each hard lick is a step toward an orgasm. I can feel myself getting closer and closer, and just when I'm sure he's going to let me fall into the abyss, he pulls away and enters me with two fingers.

Clamping down on him, I lift my hips and bite my lip, holding back the whimper of pleasure that threatens to escape. Sweat beads against my forehead, strands of hair sticking to my face. My chest heaves and my nipples harden.

I need this. I need him.

"Don't be shy... tell me how it feels... tell me what you need, baby," Zane rasps against my folds, his own desire clear in his voice.

"You... I want you." I gasp as he curves his fingers upward, almost as if he is dragging the orgasm right out of me.

"Fuck, Dove, come on my face. Let me taste you, squeeze my fingers..." He goes from licking to sucking my clit hard, and I explode, igniting into a raging inferno of pleasure. Tilting my head back into the pillows, I whimper beneath his touch, my thighs trembling, my heart racing.

My core clenches as if it has its own heartbeat, and my release gushes out and onto his face. I should be embarrassed at how fast I came apart, but I become melted chocolate in this man's hands. Eyes wide open, I stare up at the ceiling.

I haven't even come down from my high yet, and he's withdrawing his fingers. Whimpering, I want to tell him to come back, to do it all over again, but he moves to the spot beside me, resting against the headboard.

"Come here. I want you to ride me," Zane orders gruffly.

Slowly, I get my jellied body to move. As I sit up, I reach for the thick cock between his legs and lean forward, sucking the mushroom-shaped crown between my lips.

Instantly, Zane's fingers sink into my hair, tugging at the strands harshly. Each tug sends a jolt of pleasure straight to my core.

"Fucking, fuck..."

I look up at him, his cock in my mouth, and I see how vulnerable, how bare, he looks. This is Zane, the dark, psychotic criminal that would slaughter, destroy, and rip the world apart for me, and he is all mine. I'll never give him up. *Never.*

Releasing his cock, I toss a leg over his hip and straddle him. My hands move to his shoulders to steady myself while his hands move to my hips, holding me in place. My slickness slides over his hard abs, and I lift myself, guiding the head of his cock to my entrance.

Our gazes collide and stay that way as I sink down on his length, impaling myself. I can feel him deep, so deep. Feel us becoming one single eternity.

The air sizzles as our bodies come together, and our breaths mingle as we both pause, relishing in the tremors of pleasure that wrack our bodies.

"I love you," I say, sighing as I start to move up and down at a torturous pace.

"I love you more," Zane groans, and his head tips back against the headboard. He watches me through hooded eyes, his fingers digging into my hips, not guiding, but anchoring me. I love the way he's looking at me right now, like I'm his heaven, the moon, and the stars in the sky. Like I'm his everything.

"Fuck, I've never seen anything so beautiful..."

"Me either," I say, letting out a gasp as his hips flex up and the head of his cock brushes against my g-spot. I'm full, so full. I can't tell where he starts and where I end. Grinding against him, I move back and forth like a wave against the beach.

Releasing my hips, his hands roam my body, mapping out each inch of flesh, touching parts of my soul. We're frenzied, gasoline and fire, lightning and thunder, and we'll burn the world around us to the ground.

"I'm close," I whimper, tipping my head back, placing my hands against his firm chest as I ride him. He lets me take from him until I shatter like glass into a million pieces, and then he rolls us, taking from me, fucking me like an animal in heat.

Each stroke is raw and steals my breath a little more than the last. By the time Zane comes, we're both sticky with sweat, our breaths ragged, and our hearts thundering in our chests. Zane rolls off of me and pulls me into his side, our combined scents fill my nostrils while the warmth of his body seeps into mine.

I never want to leave this bed.

"There is no me without you. There is only us," Zane whispers into my hair.

"Us. Forever. For always," I croak and let my heavy eyes fall closed, knowing that tomorrow we have nothing to fear. There is no one to hide from, no one to watch for. There is only the future, and it looks a whole lot brighter now.

EPILOGUE

Dove

F
amily becomes everything when you've never had it
before. A year ago, I was all alone, living on my own, with
only one person who I thought cared about me. Lonely
didn't even begin to cover what I felt. One year later, and I've got a
whole new family. Xander and Damon have taken me in as if years
didn't separate us. They have families of their own, and I cannot
wait to share mine and Zane's happy news with them.

Zane and I got married in a tiny little ceremony three months
ago. Xander walked me down the aisle and gave me away while my
nieces threw rose petals along the way.

Being married isn't much different to dating. Zane is still as possessive as ever, not letting me out of his sight unless he absolutely has to.

Tonight we're doing our weekly Sunday dinner. Xander and Ella, Damon and Keira, and Ivan and Violet are here tonight.

Since getting to know my brothers, I've heard their stories of how they came to know their wives. I've also met their children and been told countless stories about how ruthless a father we shared.

They also shared some memories of our mother, the few nice ones they had anyway. I've come to terms with the fact that my mother was doing what she thought was best, that she did love me, but that she couldn't handle a life on the run. It seems her life was ruined long before I came along, and even though she tried to run from it, in the end, she just couldn't get away from her own demons.

Quinton rushes through the dining room, his baby sister hot on his heels, their squeals of joy cut through my thoughts. Xander reaches down and takes his daughter, Gia, into his arms.

She whines and pushes against him, trying to get away and to her brother, but he squeezes her a little tighter and peppers her adorable face with kisses before releasing her again. I can't believe that's going to be Zane and me soon.

"How is married life? I feel like I haven't seen you guys in ages," Violets asks, giving me a wink as she bounces her daughter on her knee.

"Yeah, I know. Zane has basically tied me to the bed," I joke, well half-joke, since what I've said is partially true. Every night before bed, we make love. Sometimes it's sweet, and other times, it's raw and consuming. There is nothing in this world like the love he gives and shows me.

"I mean, it's not like you're lying." Zane smirks and tugs me closer to him.

"Men." Violet shakes her head. "I swear, they can never get enough. I told Ivan I need at least two years without getting pregnant again."

I look over at Ivan, who is smiling like a fool. His love for Violet and his kids is profound. It's crazy to think that she was once his prisoner. Then again, looking back on mine and Zane's love story, we kind of came from the same thing.

"Doubt Ivan is going to let that happen," Damon says, chuckling.

"Yeah, me too." Violet rolls her eyes.

"When are you and Zane going to have a baby?" Keira, Damon's wife asks, taking a sip of her wine. Her question makes my cheeks flame, and suddenly, I feel everyone's eyes on me.

"Well, we actually had news to share with you all."

"Oh, my gosh, yes!" Ella basically jumps out of her chair. "You're pregnant, aren't you?"

I nod, unable to contain the smile that appears on my lips. "It's still early, but there is definitely a little peanut in there."

"Yes, mine," Zane growls into my ear, his teeth nipping my lobe in a possessive way. I swear, since discovering we're having a baby, he's become even more possessive and controlling.

He's currently working for Xander as a hitman. After we killed Matteo, we took over most of his territory. Xander asked me if I wanted to be in charge of it, but truthfully, I didn't have any idea what I was doing, so I told him he could run it.

"I'm happy for you, Sister," Xander exclaims, his eyes twinkling with joy. "We're building an empire of little Rossi's."

"We sure are." Ella giggles, looking up at her husband.

"What's that supposed to mean?" Violet narrows her gaze at her sister as if she can read her thoughts. Ella bites her bottom lip and looks like she's going to explode with happiness.

"Well, we would never want to ruin this moment for Dove and Zane because we're so very happy for you, but Xander and I are expecting again as well."

"I'm so happy for you two!" I say, taking a sip of my orange juice. I'm beyond happy. I feel safe, secure, and protected, but above all, I feel loved. I feel as if I've finally found my home.

Xander snickers. "There is nothing quite as delicious looking as my wife's belly, swollen with our child." Ella's face turns red as a tomato, and she shakes her head, dismissing his teasing.

Xander's phone starts ringing, and he curses when he looks at the name on the screen before hitting the green answer key.

"What can I do for you, Luke?" he barks into the phone.

All the men around the table sit up a little straighter, waiting for an order most likely. Luke says something, and Xander starts shaking his head.

"Okay, make sure you have someone on her at all times. We don't need any issues with the police, and I don't want to have to kill someone so young. Report back to me in a week and let me know how things go. If she talks before then, bring her in."

Luke says something else, and then Xander hangs up the phone. I'm tempted to ask what is going on but keep my lips pressed firmly together. It sounds like someone saw something they shouldn't have.

"That didn't sound good," Damon says.

"It wasn't good, but if anyone can keep people in line, it's Luke. Everything will be fine. I'm sure of it," he assures Damon, and dinner carries on. After we eat and say our goodbyes, Zane and I head back to our little cottage that's just outside the Rossi estate.

We walk into the house, and Zane reaches for me, tugging me into his arms. I crash into his chest, giggling. Max greets us at the door, curling his body around and between our legs.

While I was Christian's prisoner, Zane picked him up and brought him to the shelter I used to work at. They kept him for me, while we were dealing with all of this. I picked him up as soon as I could. Max purrs, but I'm too consumed by my husband to give the cat any attention right now.

Since he started working for Xander, his muscles seem even more firm, his abs more defined, and because my sex drive is through the roof, I find myself tracing those abs every night. Also, grinding against them.

"I never thought we would be here. Married and having children. My plan was always to let you live your life, to let you be happy. Never in my wildest dreams did I expect to be the man you'd choose to spend your life with."

I roll my eyes. "As if you would've let me pick anyone else."

He gives me a boyish grin. "Touché. Though truthfully, I would've eventually had to let you go. I knew someday you'd find someone."

"Yeah, that someone was you," I snort.

Zane's face turns serious, but I can feel the bulge of his cock in his jeans, pressing against my front, begging to be unleashed.

"I'm being serious here." He cups me by the cheeks. "I can't believe you're mine. My wife, and soon to be the mother of our child."

"Well, believe it. I'm yours today, tomorrow, and forever. Even back at the bunker, I knew that I wanted you. I was afraid to admit it, but I think I loved you then."

"Could've fooled me, unless love is shown by hitting someone in the head with a weight." I slap him playfully on the chest, loving that we can be so carefree now that there isn't anything to fear.

"It's the only way I could think of to escape."

Grinding his groin into my center, my thoughts swirl, turning from playful to lustful in an instant. I'm ready to climb him like a tree.

"You didn't escape then, and you won't now. You're my obsession, my heart, and my reason to breathe." His lips find mine, and I swear the world falls away. There is only him and me, the darkness of our past, a distant memory.

Sometimes the love your life is right in front of you.

Other times, he's hiding right outside your window, watching you sleep.

The End.

ALSO BY THE AUTHORS

CONTEMPORAY ROMANCE

North Woods University
The Bet
The Dare
The Secret
The Vow
The Promise
The Jock

Bayshore Rivals
When Rivals Fall
When Rivals Lose
When Rivals Love

Breaking the Rules
Kissing & Telling
Babies & Promises
Roommates & Thieves

***

DARK ROMANCE

The Blackthorn Elite
Hating You
Breaking You
Hurting You
Regretting You

The Obsession Duet
Cruel Obsession
Deadly Obsession

The Rossi Crime Family
Convict Me
Protect Me
Keep Me
Guard Me
Tame Me
Remember Me

***

EROTIC STANDALONES

Their Captive

Runaway Bride

His Gift

Beck AND Hallman

www.bleedingheartromance.com

beck.hallman@gmail.com

facebook @beckandhallman

Manufactured by Amazon.ca
Bolton, ON